©Fly

C000066694

Name: **Shizuka Torigoe**

Age: 17

School year: high school,
second year

Height: 4'10"

Hina's close friend and Ryou's
lunchtime friend and classmate.

"Tor—, what about you?"

"I'm good for now."

Name:
Ryou Takamori

Age: 17

School year: high school,
second year

Height: 5'9"

Self-proclaimed boring dude
struggling to fit in.

Name: Ai Himejima

Age: 16

School year: high school, second year

Height: 5'1"

Childhood friend of both Hina and Ryou. Transfer student and former idol.

Name:
Minami Shinohara

Age: 16

School year: high school, second year

Height: 5'6"

Former classmate of Ryou. She dated him for three days when they were in their third year of middle school.

Name:

Age:
Schoo

Heigh

A gya
deep
all th
the T

: Mana Takamori

5

l year: middle school,
            third year

t: 5'5"

ru kind of girl who cares
y about her brother. Does
e cooking and chores in
akamori home.

"Join us,
Ryou!"

Name: Hina Fushimi

Age: 17

School year: high school,
                second year

Height: 5'3"

Ryou's childhood friend
and an immensely popular,
gorgeous girl.

The Girl I Saved on the Train Turned Out to Be My Childhood Friend

4

Kennoji

Illustration by Fly

YEN
ON
New York

The Girl I Saved on the Train Turned Out to Be My Childhood Friend 4

Kennoji

Translation by Sergio Avila
Cover art by Fly

This book is a work of fiction. Names, characters, places, and incidents are the product of the author's imagination or are used fictitiously. Any resemblance to actual events, locales, or persons, living or dead, is coincidental.

CHIKAN SARESOU NI NATTEIRU S-KYU BISHOUJO WO TASUKETARA TONARI NO SEKI NO OSANANAJIMI DATTA volume 4
Copyright © 2021 Kennoji
Illustrations copyright © 2021 Fly
All rights reserved.
Original Japanese edition published in 2021 by SB Creative Corp.
This English edition is published by arrangement with SB Creative Corp., Tokyo in care of Tuttle-Mori Agency, Inc., Tokyo.

English translation © 2023 by Yen Press, LLC

Yen On
150 West 30th Street, 19th Floor
New York, NY 10001

Visit us at yenpress.com ✧ facebook.com/yenpress ✧ twitter.com/yenpress ✧ yenpress.tumblr.com ✧ instagram.com/yenpress

First Yen On Edition: September 2023
Edited by Yen On Editorial: Shella Wu
Designed by Yen Press Design: Wendy Chan

Yen On is an imprint of Yen Press, LLC.
The Yen On name and logo are trademarks of Yen Press, LLC.

The publisher is not responsible for websites (or their content) that are not owned by the publisher.

Library of Congress Cataloging-in-Publication Data
Names: Kennoji, author. | Fly, 1963- illustrator. | Avila, Sergio, translator.
Title: The girl I saved on the train turned out to be my childhood friend / Kennoji ; illustration by Fly ; translation by Sergio Avila.
Other titles: Chikan saresou ni natteiru s-kyu bishoujo wo tasuketara tonari no seki no osananajimi datta. English
Description: First Yen On edition. | New York, NY : Yen On, 2021–
Identifiers: LCCN 2021039082 | ISBN 9781975336998 (v. 1 ; pbk.) | ISBN 9781975337018 (v. 2 ; pbk.) | ISBN 9781975337032 (v. 3 ; pbk.) | ISBN 9781975368005 (v. 4 ; pbk.)
Subjects: CYAC: Love—Fiction. | LCGFT: Light novels.
Classification: LCC PZ7.1.K507 Gi 2021 | DDC [Fic]—dc23
LC record available at https://lccn.loc.gov/2021039082

ISBNs: 978-1-9753-6800-5 (paperback)
978-1-9753-6801-2 (ebook)

10 9 8 7 6 5 4 3 2 1

LSC-C

Printed in the United States of America

We decided to make an indie movie for the school festival, and script-writer Torigoe was in charge of the plot.

"I feel bad about pushing it all onto you, though," I said after taking a bite of my lunch.

The physics room was quiet, far removed from the hustle and bustle of the lunch rush.

Although we'd had a planning meeting the other day at my house, it went nowhere. In the end, we just decided to leave it all up to Torigoe.

I thought the more heads, the better, but that was not the case at all—quite the opposite. Everyone had their own idea of what would make an interesting film, and we weren't getting anywhere.

The meeting ended up becoming a party; we chatted for around two hours, then ate the dinner my sister cooked and, afterward, played games all night.

"It's fine. I don't mind," Torigoe said. "And I'm glad we had that sleepover party; I got to know what kind of story Hiina, Himeji, and you are picturing."

She grabbed another bite with her chopsticks.

Sleepover... So you see it that way, too, eh?

I guess Fushimi also wanted more of a party than a meeting.

My childhood friend, Hina Fushimi, was exceptionally popular and loved by boys and girls. Yet despite having a long list of friends, she had never been to a sleepover; she really wished to experience one.

Due to how everyone idolized her, she kept herself at a distance. She wouldn't step too far into her friends' private lives, and they wouldn't step too far into hers.

This changed once she made a new friend who she opened her heart to: the girl silently eating lunch before me, Torigoe.

"I want to make a project schedule before summer vacation."

"Right."

"Himeji seemed pretty anxious, so."

Right... I nodded, remembering what she'd said.

"Will we really make it in time?"

She had looked pretty anxious indeed.

She wasn't exasperated per se, but she was clearly worried.

By the way, Himeji refers to Ai Himejima—my other childhood friend, who just recently transferred into our school.

A couple of years ago, she used to live in the area, until she moved to Tokyo. And now she'd moved back here again... She was still very pretty, though of a different kind from Fushimi. She was an actual idol.

She had told only me, but everyone at the sleepover party, save for one person, had their suspicions about it.

So Himeji, having had experience in the production of audiovisual media, most likely said that out of concern if we'd be on schedule.

"I can help you out if you want."

"Hmm..." Torigoe held her chopsticks with her mouth while tapping at her phone; she was looking at the notes app. "I already have something, actually."

"Whoa, really? What's it about?"

"Well..."

Then the fact that Torigoe was an avid reader of Boys Love novels crossed my mind.

"H-hold on. Why the hesitation?! Are you trying to make us film something embarrassing?!"

"Wh-what?! No!" Torigoe denied frantically. "I'm just a bit self-conscious about people reading my writing. It feels like I'm letting them peer into my soul."

…Wow. I expected her to be able to detach herself from that sort of thing. Guess I was wrong.

"Then let's say I came up with it. If they don't like it, then all the criticism can fall on me."

"I feel like that's cheating."

"Who cares? I mean, we're placing too much responsibility on you as it is. And hey, it's also the director's job to take the heat for a film's reception."

Even if I suggested she talk to Fushimi or Himeji instead of me, she'd probably feel the same no matter who it was.

In any case, I had to hear her idea first if we were gonna make this movie.

"Thanks, Takamori."

"Hmm? Uh…okay?"

Why am I being thanked?

Torigoe noticed my confusion, so she continued:

"I feel better about it now. I only have some notes still, but I'll organize them into something I can show by the end of the school day."

"Take your time. No rush."

"No, I want to do it now."

The conversation seemed to have lit a fire inside her—she continued to type on her phone, forgetting all about her lunch.

She kept this up even after returning to the classroom. Next period was held in a different place, but she just sat at her desk with no intention of going anywhere.

She realized she had to leave only when Fushimi called out to her. She grabbed her textbook and notebook, and the two left the classroom.

Himeji and I followed behind, making our way to the biology lab.

"This is your fault, just so you know," I said.

Himeji frowned. "Why me?"

"Because you're in such a hurry," I replied while still looking ahead.

I heard a sigh from beside me.

"You realize we only have roughly two weeks left until summer vacation? We need to decide roles for everyone in class and have them prepare stuff during the break."

...She's right.

Himeji's shapely face grimaced upon seeing the look of agreement on mine.

"This is *your* job, Mr. Director."

"Sorry. I'm still learning the ropes."

Give this newbie a break.

Himeji was super strict. On other people and probably on herself, too.

"Thanks for the advice. I'll keep it in mind."

She immediately brightened up. Then quickly looked away so I wouldn't notice.

"You don't have to...thank me."

This girl. You can just say, You're welcome.

"Ryou, Ai, hurry up! We'll be late!" Fushimi turned around and waved at us, so we hurried to the lab.

Despite Torigoe's intention, she wasn't able to organize her notes by the end of the school day.

"I'll let you know as soon as I'm done," she told me while I was writing the class journal, then left right away.

"Was that about the screenplay?" Fushimi asked me with a curious expression, all the while spell-checking my logs.

"Yeah, she's been organizing her ideas since lunchtime."

"And she's not done yet?"

I shook my head.

"That's important, too, yes, but don't forget we have tests coming up." Fushimi looked happy for whatever reason.

She had been playing the part of my tutor for a while now, and thanks to that, I'd been getting comparatively good grades on the quizzes.

©Fly

My grades were poor... I mean, I had plenty of space to improve, so after Professor Hina began tutoring me, they jumped up quite a bit, relatively, compared to where they were before.

"It is time to show the fruits of your labor!"

"I sure hope I see some fruit."

Why are you so excited about it anyway?

"Waka was complimenting you on your progress, remember?"

"Yeah, I guess."

Waka—Miss Wakatabe—was our English and homeroom teacher.

On our last quiz, she'd taken me by surprise. She usually chewed me out, but this time, she'd clapped. "Bravo!" she'd said.

"I was so happy when I saw that." She beamed like the warm spring sun.

Looks like I made my childhood friend realize the delights of teaching.

Honestly...there's not much to be delighted about. I'm still in deep trouble.

Fushimi flipped through the pages of a planner she had pulled out of her bag.

She opened her calendar to July. The page was covered in notes: exam period, school breaks...

Right, summer break's soon.

What did I do last year? I think I played games all day; then I...I... Oh man, I don't remember anything else.

It appeared I had spent my last summer break a bit too leisurely—enough so as to not remain in my mind.

We finished up the journal entry, then closed the doors as we left the classroom.

"Do you have any plans for summer vacation?" Fushimi asked as she stared at me.

"Huh? Well... We're shooting the film, aren't we?"

"Oh! You're right!" She clapped her hands together in realization, then put on a serious look. "We're going to do this properly. It's gonna be my magnum opus."

"Wow, that's some passion. Too much, in fact. We haven't even started yet."

She was ready to sprint at top speed from the very beginning.

"We need at least this much passion!"

Okay... I foresee weariness in my future.

Fushimi started talking enthusiastically about film theory this and acting theory that. It all went in one ear and out the other as we handed the journal to Waka and left the school grounds.

"It's gonna be your magnum opus! And mine! Our masterpiece!" was the conclusion of all that.

Everyone nearby gave us weird looks thanks to Fushimi's loud and excited voice.

Her engine was going full throttle before things even began. It was smoking. *Well, she did suggest we make this in the first place.*

"It will," I replied in a monotone. Fushimi paid no mind, and I ended up listening to her talk about our indie film the entire way home.

This was probably what it meant to be passionate about something to the point of losing track of time.

She kept talking about it to the very last second, until she closed the front door to her house.

It was rare to see Fushimi being so talkative like this.

I guess this is just her secret wish.

I thought back and wondered if I ever had something like that.

"...Nope. Nothing," I muttered on the short walk back home.

Something to be passionate about.

Something I loved to death.

Something I wanted to talk about with someone else.

Something...

"I wish I had that sort of passion."

"Huh?!"

I turned around to the voice and found my sister, Mana, pushing her bike.

"B-Bubby... looking for passion?!"

"I think you're misunderstanding something... And why're you following me?"

"Well, we live in the same direction."

True.

Like always, Mana had her middle school uniform's skirt rolled all the way up. She wore her shoulder bag like a backpack. In her bike's basket were eco bags full of food she'd just bought at the supermarket.

"I kept calling out to you, but you just ignored me. Bad Bubby."

"How many times do I have to tell you not to call me that in public?"

"What's wrong with it? It's cute."

No, it's not.

"So, so, so? What were you talking about?" She drew her face close to mine, her eyes lighting up with excitement.

"I was just talking to myself. Don't mind it."

"Whaaa—? C'mooon!" She pouted, then started booing at me.

"...What about you, Mana? Is there something you're passionate about?"

"Me? Of course!"

"Huh? What?"

"Cooking."

An unbecoming thing to say for a *gyaru*. But indeed, her cooking was quite scrumptious.

"Why do you think that is?"

"Because it's fun...?"

"Bzzzt! Nope!"

Mana cooked our meals pretty much every day. She also chewed me out any time I tried to use any of the food in the fridge.

"Why do you like cooking, then?"

"Because I love seeing you enjoy my food." She giggled, then got on her bike and rode away.

I had a feeling dinner would be as wonderful as always that night, too.

Although Torigoe said she'd tell me as soon as she finished, I had yet to receive any text. I figured she was still having trouble wrapping things up, but then...

"Good evening."

She came to my house.

My jaw dropped when I opened the door. I glanced at the clock in the hallway before looking back at her.

"Good evening...? You do realize it's past ten, right?"

"Yeah. I had to do some chores and didn't have the time to finish until now."

"We could've talked tomorrow."

"I mean, yes, but I wanted you to hear it as soon as possible."

Seeing that she was ready to share, I took her to my room and got her some tea.

Mana was taking a bath, by the way. She would have gotten the door in my place if it weren't for that, and she'd have fainted at the entrance, probably.

"It's still pretty messy," Torigoe said before delving into the details.

Her idea cleared the biggest hurdles: a story that we could realize within our tight budget and limited skillset.

"Wh-what do you think?"

The explanation took about fifteen minutes, since I kept asking questions. Our cups of tea were already empty by then.

"Sounds good. It'll make a good movie."

"R-really? Oh, I'm so glad to hear that."

Torigoe had felt shy about sharing her idea, and her voice had been really soft at the beginning, but it gradually got louder and louder.

"Fushimi would be perfect as the protagonist, too. Would Himeji be okay as the rival?"

"Yeah, I don't think there's anyone better."

I nodded in agreement.

Torigoe's story was about a high school girl, and it focused on her youth, romance, and club activities. The plot wasn't anything intense, and it fit with the planned format of the short film.

"Hiina and Himeji are friends but also rivals…"

"And they both fall in love with the same guy…"

Torigoe glanced at me.

"But we're not showing the guy, huh."

"Yup. We're deliberately taking him out," she replied.

He was part of the story but had no time in the limelight. It focused on their rivalry instead.

"I'm just worried that Himeji's terrible acting will stand out even more in contrast with Hiina's great work."

"…" I pictured it before speaking. "Sure, it might be obvious at some points, but it'll be fine."

"You think?"

"Yeah, she doesn't have to do much to make a good impression on-screen. It'll work out."

She was a former idol, after all. *But don't tell Himeji I said that.*

There was no one else with as much acting experience as Fushimi anyway, so we couldn't be too picky. Besides, the role was perfect for that competitive girl.

Although Himeji was hiding the fact that she used to be an idol, rumors would probably start spreading once people caught wind of her appearance in the movie.

Then Torigoe asked for more of my opinions.

"Oh, I see." "Okay, then let's do this." She took notes of everything on her phone.

Then, in the middle of our very productive meeting, I heard the door open just a few inches.

"…"

Mana peeked in. She did a double-take once she noticed who was with me.

"Wha—?! Shizu!"

She no longer cared about hiding and opened the door theatrically and came in.

Her hair was still slightly damp, and she had a towel on her shoulders.

"Sorry for bothering you so late at night."

"No, it's fine, it's fine."

She glared at me. Her eyes were demanding an explanation.

"She's here to talk about the movie. We're finalizing ideas for the script."

"And it couldn't wait until tomorrow?"

"I guess not. But really, what's the harm in coming this…late…?" I glanced at the clock; it was way past eleven. "T-Torigoe!"

"Wh-what?"

"When's the last train? You came by train, right?"

"The last…? Oh."

She had totally forgotten about it.

She looked it up on her phone and found the time right away.

"It's leaving in eight minutes."

I immediately jumped up.

"If we bike there, we might just make it in time!"

"Huh? Why not just stay for the night?"

"We've got school tomorrow, remember?" I rebuked Mana.

Torigoe nodded. "Yeah, I don't have my uniform… I gotta go."

Torigoe started packing her stuff while Mana simply watched.

"Y'know, Hina's gonna pass out if she hears Shizu stayed overnight. Like, she'll have foam coming out of her mouth," Mana said nonchalantly.

"Don't be so dramatic."

Although…actually…I can picture her dark smile when she finds out…

"Oh. Wow. Sounds fun. Did you have fun? You must've had so much fun," she'd say.

"Yeah, and we don't want that. At all."

Mana looked as if she had more to say, but we paid her no mind and left the house. I grabbed my bike's handlebar and kicked off the stand.

"Can you ride behind?"

"W-we're both going?"

"Yeah."

"I—I can't."

"…What?"

"But I guess I'll make an effort."

"Yes, please."

I straddled the bike, and she softly placed her hands on my hips.

"L-like this?"

"Anywhere's fine—just hold on tight. We're going."

Once I saw her sit down, I pedaled as fast as I could.

I heard her giggle behind me.

"Hee-hee. You're really going *'uwoooh,'* like they do in manga."

"H-hey! Don't make me laugh. You'll make me slow down."

"I'm just stating the facts."

She must've found it really hilarious—she kept on giggling for a while.

"Ahhh! Hey, wait!"

"What?"

"My sandal fell off."

"What?! Seriously?!" I slammed the brakes.

"Bweeeh!"

I heard a strange scream; then something hit my back. It was probably Torigoe's face.

"I'll go get it," she said.

She hopped on one foot all the way to where the sandal had fallen off. She put it back on, then hopped onto the bike again, and I pedaled hard.

But then I had this strange feeling.

I was trying to catch my breath as I watched Torigoe run into the station, and just as I turned my bike to take my sweet time heading home, she came back.

She looked incredibly regretful.

"S-sorry... I couldn't make it in time."

"I figured."

"We would've made it if I hadn't lost my sandal back there."

"No, I don't think it would've mattered."

"I don't have money for a taxi... So I'll just wait for the first train here."

"No, no. Mana wanted you to stay over, so we can just come back when it's time for the first train."

She shook her head.

"I've already caused you enough trouble."

She tucked in her neck deeper and deeper; it looked like she was shrinking.

"What am I even doing? We could've talked tomorrow. I got too excited, bothered you late at night, made you bring me here, and then I made you stop because I couldn't keep a sandal on my darn foot, and because of that we were late, and now I'm troubling you even more..."

She was in full-on negative mode.

"I don't think it's a bother."

Despite my reassurance, she still kept her head lowered.

"Where was your house again?"

"Huh? My house?"

She gave me her address and the nearest station.

"So it's about an hour away by bike."

Thankfully, I had my phone on me, so the maps app would prevent us from getting lost.

"It's also my fault for not realizing you had to be back before the last train. If you want, I can take you home."

I tapped the bike's handle.

"Really? I-I'll let you know, unlike Hina, I'm a big ball of mass, y'know? I'm heavy. I guess you must've realized that by now, but the distance is much longer this time…"

"'Big ball of mass'? What's that supposed to mean?" I laughed. "And what about you? Your butt will be hurting after such a long trip."

Torigoe didn't say anything, and just sat back on the bike's cargo rack.

I started pedaling, and after a minute or so, I realized we could just wait for my mom to come back and ask her to take Torigoe home. I put forward the idea, but…

"I don't think I could ask her to do that. I don't want to bother her."

Rather than being modest, it felt like she just had trouble asking others for help. In any case, she really regretted missing the last train.

Apparently, her family couldn't come pick her up, either. She said she'd come here without telling anyone.

"So I can't call them. Sorry."

"I guess we've got no choice."

Torigoe gave me directions by looking at the maps app. I biked wherever she told me to go.

We passed the well-illuminated national highway, then our school's neighborhood, and we talked about the movie on our way to her house.

"So how are we gonna end the movie? You said you weren't sure."

Since the story was about two girls falling in love with the same guy...

"Maybe we could end it without either of them winning, but then again, that might feel too cliché..."

In shounen manga, usually the protagonist would defeat the rival.

"I'll make it so the story could go either way."

"That sounds best."

"By the way, Takamori, you doing okay? Am I not heavy?"

"I told you—it's fine." She had asked the same thing many times already. "You're too thin to worry about that in the first place."

"Still, I can't help it," she whispered.

"Oh, take a left there." "Now go straight until the next light." She gave me instructions in a monotone, like she was the app's voice navigator.

Then it was silent.

We never talked much to begin with. We usually spent time together in silence.

"Be honest," she said. There was a long pause before she talked again. "...What do you think of Hiina?"

What do I think of her?

I pondered on how to convey my thoughts without creating any misunderstandings, but she got annoyed by the silence.

"Sorry. Forget about it."

"O-okay..."

"I mean, I'm not really sure if I wanna know..."

She sounded confused.

It was late at night but still early July. Rainy season was almost over. And having to ride a bike for so long in this humidity had me worrying about something.

"Torigoe, I don't think you should cling to me that much."

"Why?"

"I'm sweating."

"Yeah. It's fine."

"No, it's not fine."

"I won't say you smell good, but hey, I don't hate it."

How am I supposed to take that?

She ignored my demands and took her hands off the rack and held me tight. I felt her cheek against my back, her warmth through my T-shirt.

"It's so warm."

"That much is true." I sighed.

"You know, I really, really love…"

My body froze up as I waited for her to continue.

"…this time of day."

Oh, that's what you meant. Oof.

"You thought I was talking about you?"

"…N-no."

"Okay." She giggled.

By the time I came back home, it was already two in the morning. It was only then that I noticed Mana had sent me a barrage of texts: Did she make it?! Hey!! Answer me!!! OH MY GODDD!!!!!

I was scared to hear what she'd say when she woke up.

I took a shower, then looked up some stuff on my phone in bed until I passed out. It was ten in the morning by the time I woke up.

"…Wait."

Ten? AM?

Wasn't it a school day?

I checked and the alarms on my phone had rung. But I had not heard any of them.

Then I saw a note, in Fushimi's handwriting, saying: *I'm going without you, Sleeping Beauty! More like Sleeping Dummy!*

"Don't know which adjective I prefer to be called."

Apparently, she had come by, and I still couldn't wake up.

"School…"

I put my barely awake brain to work.

We...don't have English today. No Waka. So maybe I could just take the day off.

I stopped reaching out for my uniform and fell back down onto the bed.

I opened the browser on my phone and saw the tabs I had opened last night.

"..."

I had been researching stuff about shooting films. I looked into the tools and devices we'll need and read blogs and bios about people who had filmed indie movies. I was starting to get an idea of what it entailed.

"I think I need a PC for this..."

Up until now, I had edited videos on my phone, but it looked like it wouldn't be optimal for this project.

But I didn't have the money to buy a computer...

I groaned, pensive, when I heard the doorbell.

Probably a delivery?

I went downstairs, still in my pajamas, and opened the door. Himeji was standing outside, wearing her school uniform.

"Whoa. Himeji...what are you doing here?"

"Ryou! Shouldn't you be in bed?!"

She seemed to be panicking.

"Oh, no. I was asleep until just now, actually."

"Oh, really? Sorry for waking you up. Excuse me," she said as she pushed me aside to enter.

"Himeji, what about school?"

"I slipped out."

"Why...?"

"Shizuka said you might be feeling unwell. She was pretty sad, you know? So I came to nurse you back to health."

Torigoe...? I guess she thinks I got sick after taking her home so late or something.

"You don't have to, so just go back to school, Himeji. I'm fine."

She placed a paper bag full of food on the kitchen counter, then waggled her finger with a smug look.

"Hey, we've been friends forever. I can tell what you're actually thinking, and it's that you really want me to take care of you."

"Are you being serious with that?"

She washed her hands, then grabbed her phone.

"Can you even cook?"

"Yes, I just need to follow the video."

"So you can't."

"Geez! You go back to bed. I'll bring the food to you once it's done."

If it's done.

"I don't need to be taken care of; I'm not sick…"

"Yeah, yeah. I know how kind you really are; you're just saying that to not worry me."

"No, listen…"

She's not listening…

Himeji ignored me and put on an apron.

I gave up trying to convince her and went back to my room to wait for the completed product.

I changed clothes and grabbed my phone.

I tried looking up part-time jobs for high schoolers during summer vacation.

A bunch of results popped up, but I wasn't sure I'd be able to do well in any of them.

Maybe I could get someone else to lend me their computer?

"No…" I shook my head.

I wanted to do this myself, not rely on someone.

Thankfully, we hadn't started filming. I had time. If I needed to ask for help, the time wasn't now, when we hadn't even started.

"…She's sure taking her time."

It had been thirty minutes already.

I really couldn't picture Himeji being a good cook. I'd been with her during cooking class in grade school, and she just ignored anything the textbook or the teacher said and tried making her own concoctions.

I've got a bad feeling about this...

"Hey, Himeji?" I peered into the kitchen.

She was stirring a pot as she hummed.

"It's almost done." She turned around with a big smile.

In contrast to her bright expression, the kitchen was in shambles. It looked as if a wild cat had passed through and wreaked havoc.

I'm in trouble...

I nearly fainted at the sight. Mana would be so furious.

"Okay, I'll clean up. You finish making that."

"Yes, sir!"

Himeji kept on merrily stirring as I washed the scattered utensils and put seasonings back where they belonged.

I tried taking a peek of the scary pot's contents and saw it bubbling.

"Uh..." There were actual, transparent, rainbow-colored bubbles. This couldn't be right. "Himejima, you did follow the instructions to the letter, right?"

"Yes, of course," she replied with a beaming smile.

"And in the, um, in the video, did you see bubbles like these? You know, shining bubbles reflecting all colors of the rainbow...as though you mixed in detergent?"

"No, but I'm sure it's just a tiny detail. A small miscalculation."

Uh-oh...

"Did you wash the ingredients properly?"

"You're such a worrywart. Yes, I did. They didn't show that step in the video, though, but I know how to wash things." She grabbed the dish-washing liquid from the sink. "I used dish soap, duh."

All strength left my knees.

She looked so happy, I couldn't correct her...

I couldn't tell her that wasn't edible.

Himeji finished her detergent soup and poured it into a bowl, then nodded in satisfaction.

"Hee-hee. Just like in the video."

I doubt that.

I wanted to take back my statement about not being sick...because I was soon about to become ill.

"Himeji, you know, tutorials aren't some sort of unrelenting god. Sometimes you gotta use your own judgment..."

"Ryou, you really don't know? Gods are real, and they are on the Internet."

"I don't think you get what I mean."

She had clearly cooked for only one. She placed the bowl on the table and sat in the seat across with a huge grin.

"Go ahead."

"What about you?"

"Oh, I have my own lunch."

Lucky...

Guess I'll just drink a bunch of water afterward.

I scooped a spoonful of soup, closed my eyes tight, and shoved it into my mouth.

"How is it? Tasty, right?"

How in the world are you so confident?

"...Is this consommé? Oh, but there's a citrusy smell ...like the fragrance of detergent..."

Himeji tilted her head.

"That's weird. I didn't put any citrus in there."

Yes, you did. The darn detergent.

There was a slight tinge of dish soap—but it didn't taste that bad overall.

I drank three glasses of water for every spoonful of soup.

I should take some stomach medicine, too, just in case.

"...So, about that one thing," Himeji said, finally getting to the topic she wanted to discuss.

"What thing?"

"The promise in the notebook. Just before I moved away...you...and I...we were both...in love..." Her voice got quieter as she went on.

Her awkwardness just made me feel awkward about it, too.

"B-back then! We were, back then!"

"Yes, of course." She cast her eyes down, red in the face.

Dealing with her when she was like this, so unlike her usual self, was tough...

In my notebook from third grade, there was a love umbrella with my and Himeji's names, plus our promise written inside.

The problem was that it was the same promise Fushimi had told me about.

"I think Hina tried using my promise as hers, taking advantage of the fact that I was moving away."

"Or maybe I just forgot about it."

"Or maybe Hina is lying."

It was quite probable that I simply didn't remember it.

"I think I just forgot. I mean, I barely remember anything about grade school."

"Hina's...clever. Cunning. I can't discard the possibility that she's using my promise to her advantage." She furrowed her brow.

In my notebook from fifth grade, there was a note, in girly handwriting, that said, *"When we get into high school, I'll have my first kiss with Hina."*

If Fushimi herself had written that, and she did just as Himeji feared, then...

"She might be manipulating you, taking advantage of the fact that you've forgotten everything."

"Manipulating me for what? Not like I have any money or fame or power."

"It might be nothing big for you…but it is…for Shizuka and me."

Yet there was no way to prove it was true unless Fushimi confessed to it.

"Can't we just consider these as separate issues?"

"You're too nice to her, Ryou."

There was this sadness to her eyes when she glanced at me.

"Do you feel good, being so close to someone popular?"

"I've never thought of it like that," I said.

"…Sorry. I shouldn't have said that."

"Don't worry." I shook my head.

There were probably people who saw it like that, out of envy.

But we only returned to our current relationship after I saved her on the train. That was entirely coincidental, and not something you could plan. Besides, I hadn't even known she was the victim.

"I was pretty popular, too, remember?"

"Yeah, you sure worked hard as an idol."

"I did. Yet, she's taken you from me…" She looked up at me. "…And you liked me first…"

I replied with a chuckle and told her that's in the past, but she pursed her lips and closed her eyes.

"I-I'm going back to school."

"Huh? Uh…okay?"

She stood right up and grabbed her bag, then hurried over to the door. Before she could close it all the way, I opened it back up.

"Himeji. Thank you for taking care of me today."

She glanced back, then stuck out her tongue. She looked away, her face beet red, and ran away.

◆Shizuka Torigoe◆

"I wonder where Ai went."

Hiina was pressing the top of her mechanical pencil against her cheek as she looked around.

I was sitting at the desk next to hers. The owner of the seat hadn't come to school yet, and the teacher wasn't there, either.

"I guess she's playing hooky."

Himeji was more of a slacker than she appeared.

Hiina immediately grimaced.

"She should really be doing this worksheet—it'll be useful for the test."

"You're the only one who's that serious about tests." I chuckled.

She frowned, as though she couldn't understand why.

"Do you think you'll do well on your tests?" Hiina asked.

"Yeah. Like always."

"Oh, okay then." She smiled.

The conversation ended there all of a sudden. I didn't think this was what she really wanted to talk about.

It was during the break after first period that we started worrying about Takamori being absent.

"Where's Ryou?"

"I dropped by his house this morning, and he wouldn't wake up. In the end, I left without him."

It was then that I first heard how Hiina visited Takamori's house every morning.

"Mana and I tried our best to wake him up, but it was useless."

"Oh, is that so? He really sleeps like a log, huh?"

I just listened to their conversation.

Every time I visited, I painstakingly fixed my hair and chose nice clothes; meanwhile, Hiina was casually dropping by every morning.

What was special to me was commonplace for her.

I supposed with their houses being in the same neighborhood, it probably felt similar to dropping by a convenience store... *Unfair childhood-friend advantage.*

"He's not even reading my texts," Himeji said.

"Nor mine. Ughhh. Is he planning on staying home all day?" Hiina glared at her phone as she complained.

"I think Takamori's feeling unwell."

Note, I did not say, *Maybe he's feeling unwell.* No. I said, *"I think he's feeling unwell."*

I realized my poor choice of words too late. I didn't like how it sounded as if I was competing to see who knew him better.

But it could also be true; if anything was to be blamed for his absence, it was because of what had happened last night.

I'd missed the last train and made him take me all the way home on bike.

I was happy about his actions, but I'd feel really bad if he got sick because of it.

"He was in perfect health yesterday, though. But you think he's feeling unwell?" Himeji tilted her head.

"Um, yeah. I wonder if he's got a fever."

"No way—Ryou only ever misses school specifically when he's in good health," Hiina said.

"I'm just stating the possibilities. It's not like I know for sure."

"It doesn't sound too out there."

Himeji then left the classroom. We thought she went to the restroom, but she wasn't back by the time the next class began.

"Did she go to the infirmary?" Hiina asked.

"You think she's feeling sick, too?"

"Ai's not much of a team player, you know. She always acts on her own and never communicates."

I glanced at the seat on the other side of Hiina.

Himeji was certainly unpredictable to me.

One time, I saw two girls asking her if she wanted to go to the restroom together, and she declined. The girls glanced at each other awkwardly and walked away.

I got culture shock from seeing that.

I didn't have the courage to do that. Even if I had nothing to talk about with them, I would have immediately given in and gone with them. Then I'd join whatever they were doing while I looked in the mirror. Whether if it was to talk about class, a teacher, popular videos on the web, people they didn't like, or anything else.

Hiina kept working on the worksheet as she added, "Ai's a lone wolf. I think that's amazing."

One could call herself someone's friend once she went with them to the restroom.

So what? you may ask, but you see, you need that sort of label, otherwise the relationship becomes unclear.

I think it's similar to the same reason why couples kiss each other. Not like I could know for sure, though, since I'd never had a boyfriend.

"Shii, you done?"

"Almost."

"Let's go to the restroom once you finish."

"Okay."

I finished solving the last problem and flipped the sheet over and grabbed my handkerchief. We talked about how hard the worksheet was as we got up from our seats and walked through the silent hallways.

"I wonder what's up with Ryou."

"I hope he's just playing hooky."

"Hmm, I don't think that'd be good, either." Hiina put on an awkward smile. "Why do you think he's feeling unwell anyway?"

My choice of words must have remained on her mind this whole time, like a pebble inside her sneaker.

"Last night, I went to his house. We talked about the movie, and then I missed the last train."

"…Oh."

Her smile became strained.

"So he took me home on his bike."

"Wha—?! All the way to your house? That's so far."

"Yeah. I'm really grateful he did that, but I think he got back home real late, so…"

"I see. In that case, I'm sure he's just sleeping in super late."

"I hope so."

I shouldn't have told her the truth.

I could've easily said I assumed, since he wasn't reading his texts, that he was likely still in bed.

There was no need for me to tell the truth.

I just caught Hiina in my bout of jealousy.

"…I'm sorry."

"Why? Don't apologize. It's his fault for being a sleepyhead."

Hiina put on a bright smile.

No. I'm not apologizing about that.

I couldn't say it, though.

"So what's the movie going to be about?"

She noticed my cloudy expression and tried changing the subject.

"We only have the rough outline, but…"

Hiina listened intently to my explanation.

I apologized once again, in my head.

It was time for exams.

Fushimi, Himeji, Torigoe, and I were studying at the library when Shinohara came by after hearing about it.

Himeji was sitting next to me, while Fushimi sat across the table.

Shinohara and Torigoe were studying at the table next to ours.

"Shii, what've you been doing this whole time?" Shinohara asked as she put down her pen.

"I'm working on the screenplay. I'm in the zone right now."

"You're not studying?" She furrowed her brow in concern.

"I'll be fine," Torigoe said.

"Ryou, eyes back here. Finish your worksheet."

I languidly replied in understanding. She must've heard about the screenplay, too, since she was also curiously glancing at Torigoe.

"Hina, if you're that interested, you should just go over there and have her show it to you," Himeji said with her eyes still on her workbook.

Fushimi shook her head. "I'm studying now."

Torigoe's grades weren't that good. If she didn't get at least thirty points in math and English on the upcoming tests, she'd have to take remedial courses during summer break. Which was why Professor Hina was helping her out with mainly those two subjects.

"Ai, you got that wrong…"

"Don't mind me. Focus on your own studying."

"I won't fail a subject no matter what; it's okay."

©Fly

Tremendous confidence.

…I wish that were me.

Himeji seemed to think the same; she glanced back at her smiling childhood friend with furrowed brows.

"Speaking of which, were you the smart type, Himeji?"

"I'm smarter than you, that much is sure."

I tried recalling what she was like in grade school, when I saw what looked to be an answer sheet peeking out from within her notebook.

Is that the last math quiz we had…?

I looked for an opening as she concentrated on solving the problems in her workbook and snatched the sheet of paper.

Out of a total score of fifty, there was a big red three written on it.

"Pfft! You're worse than I am!"

Himeji then noticed what happened and grabbed the quiz back.

"Hey! Who gave you permission to look at that?!"

"C'mon, Himeji. Come. On."

"Wipe that grin off your darn face…"

"Geez. Wanna know my score on that quiz, Miss Smarter Than Me?"

I didn't wait for her answer and pulled out my own.

"Thirteen."

"No… It can't be… This huge difference is unreal…" She gritted her teeth.

Fushimi rolled her eyes.

"You didn't reach the passing grade of thirty percent, either, Ryou. You failed."

"Don't drag me back to painful reality. Y'know, if you just doubled it, then I'd get a twenty-six… Oh man… Twenty-six…"

That's amazing.

"What are you happy about? Get out of la-la land, Ryou. You failed."

"I'm just saying, if you doubled your own score, it'd be six. Get it? I'm twenty points above you."

"No way... Th-the humiliation...!"

"Didn't you take an exam before transferring in?"

"I did, but it was multiple-choice, so I had no problem."

Fushimi cleared her throat then.

"In this world, there are only two kinds of people: those who fail and those who pass. I'm the latter. What about you?" She grinned. "So stop comparing your failures and concentrate on studying, okay?"

"Fine." "Yes." We answered in unison.

I regained my focus and was answering problems in my workbook when Himeji quickly stopped again. I glanced at her profile and saw her shapely eyebrows and nose and her peach-colored lips twisted in a frown.

"Takaryou, stop staring at Lady Aika."

Before I knew it, Shinohara had changed places with Fushimi.

"I am not."

She looked at me as though I were a bug flying around fruit.

"Minami." Himeji called her name.

Shinohara straightened her back immediately. "Yesh?! Wh-what is the matter?"

"My name is Ai Himejima. I'd appreciate if you could call me that." She put on her professional smile.

"I—I could never dare utter your true name, Lady Aika..."

"Um..." Her smile froze.

She clearly didn't know how to react to that.

"Shinohara, stop treating her like she's some sort of goddess. She doesn't enjoy it."

Shinohara pushed her glasses up and smirked.

"I'll stop you right there. Don't act as though only you understand her, just because you've known her longer. I've liked her for much longer."

"That was not my intention."

Besides, she's my childhood friend... I don't think you can know a person for much longer than that.

I think it's time I showed her there's nothing worth admiring about her.

I pointed at Himeji with my thumb.

"Listen. This goddess of yours? She scored a three on a math quiz. She's taking remedial lessons for sure, so…"

"Hey, don't tell her that." She jabbed me in my side with her elbow.

"Lady Aika flustered…angry… She's so cute no matter how… Absolutely glorious…"

Enough of the worshipping!

"Just call her Himeji. It doesn't feel like her real name, right?"

Even Torigoe was calling her that.

"Lady Hime, then."

You're not dropping the "Lady," huh?

"Yes, that is fine. Just approach me casually and don't call me Aika. It's not my name, and it's got nothing to do with me… Nothing."

That was a strong emphasis.

Since she'd have to see her more frequently from now on, I figured it would be good to have Shinohara get used to being around Himeji, so I had an idea.

"Shinohara, you're smart, aren't you? Why don't you teach her math?"

She stared back at me, as if asking, *Can I?!*

I glanced at Himeji, and while she did seem troubled, she accepted.

"Please do, Minami."

"O-okay. I—I will."

Himeji asked some questions, and Shinohara answered nervously.

Even though we go to different schools, it's good that we use the same textbook.

I looked at the next table over and saw Fushimi interrogating Torigoe.

"So what happens next, Shii?"

"I'll, um, tell you later."

Fushimi was really curious about the script; she kept trying to take a peek, changing angles desperately for a glance at the screenplay in Torigoe's hands.

"I think we could…"

"Gosh, leave me alone already… I can't focus." Torigoe pushed Fushimi's face away.

No peace at either table, huh.

It soon became closing time, and we had to leave the library.

According to Torigoe, the screenplay was about 40 percent done.

As long as there were no big changes later, we could start assigning roles and deciding on props and locations.

"I'm nearly done with the first draft. Could you give it a read once it's finished?"

I immediately agreed. "Yeah, sure."

"Shii, what about me? Hmm?"

"You have no sense of objectivity, Hiina. Wait for the final product."

"Whaaa—?"

By now, you should know what happened next: Fushimi puffed her cheeks and remained that way on the entire trip home.

As the film production progressed, summer vacation approached.

"Got anything to say?"

Fushimi had been in a bad mood the whole day. She was sitting across from me with her arms folded.

She must have been wanting to interrogate Torigoe, Himeji, and me the whole time.

We were at a fast-food restaurant by the station. She heaved a heavy sigh.

"Why did you all fail your tests? After how much we studied together?!" she inquired with a prickly tone.

We all looked at one another.

"Still, Fushimi. I got a twenty-five. I put up a good fight," I said.

Fushimi's shoulders drooped.

"How can you say that with a straight face?"

I'd barely avoided failing English, but all three of us had failed math.

"Shii. I asked you so many times if you were going to be okay."

"Yeah, and I totally thought I'll get at least a thirty."

"See, you should've aimed for a higher score in case… This is why you failed…"

"But on the upside, I finished the screenplay."

"Seriously?!" Fushimi leaned forward, her eyes shining bright, but soon shook her head to focus on the matter at hand. "Let's talk about that later… Now, Ai."

"I think I would've been more serious about it had it been multiple-choice—"

"Hey, you gotta be serious either way," I interjected.

I doubted she would've gotten better grades even then.

"I can't waste my full power on every little thing."

"Yeah, like your full power could've saved you."

"Don't get so haughty just because you got fifteen points higher than me." She huffed.

"Hiina, we won't have remedial classes as long as we score at least fifty points on the makeup test. Don't get so mad."

"I'm not mad about that; I'm mad that you didn't study enough." Fushimi sighed like a boiling teapot.

On the other hand, I was feeling optimistic. I had past experience—I was undefeated in makeup tests. I was a veteran in this line of work.

Just as Fushimi was about to continue chewing us out, Torigoe grabbed her bag and took out four stapled bundles of paper.

"I made copies of the screenplay in the staff room. This is it."

I had taken a look at it a few times throughout the process, but I never had to give much input. I thought it was well written.

Fushimi and Himeji started reading intently in silence, and Torigoe's face stiffened.

"Seeing you guys read it in front of me makes me nervous…"

Despite not even being a ten-minute read, the two kept looking it over.

Meanwhile, Torigoe got juice and quickly finished it—she clearly couldn't stand the silence.

She took out an A4-size piece of paper, and the two of us wrote down things we needed for filming. Afterward, we asked the other two to check if anything was missing. They said it was all there.

"So what did you think?" I asked in Torigoe's place, since she wasn't doing it.

"I find it interesting that the guy never shows up. That's a pretty good choice," Fushimi said.

Yeah, I don't think we'd find an actor handsome enough for you two outside the best agencies.

"For sure, this would make for better pacing for the short film," Himeji said.

"Yeah."

"And his appearance is left up to one's imagination."

They both seemed to like it.

Then we talked about the production side of things. We decided what each of our classmates' roles should be. This wouldn't have been possible without Fushimi. Thanks to her popularity, she got along well with others and knew what would suit each one of them. She knew who got along with whom and where to put an extra-serious person so they wouldn't just fool around all the time. Torigoe and I left her in charge of casting.

We decided to announce the roles during homeroom the next day and wrap it up for now.

Although roles were assigned, we had to figure out the equipment.

Maybe we could do without big lights, but we needed at least some small ones, along with a camera and mics. According to my research, we needed equipment that could cost us a few thousand yen.

I explained this to Fushimi and Himeji on our way home.

"Oh, just that much? I can pay for it," Himeji said.

"H-hold on. We can't have that."

Right. She was earning quite a bit until just recently.

"Why not?"

Fushimi shook her head in agreement with me. "He's right; we can't have you take care of it all."

Since the entire budget was needed for production itself, we had nothing left for the shooting equipment.

We had to do something about it ourselves.

"Let's work! We'll get part-time jobs over the summer. That's what us high schoolers do, right?"

"I have no idea why you would want to put yourselves through that... But I'm not getting a summer job, okay?" Himeji coldly replied to Fushimi's suggestion.

Either way, I needed to buy myself a computer and video-editing software. I supposed it was inevitable.

"What sort of work should we do?" Fushimi asked cheerily.

"I don't think there are many options for high schoolers over just summer break," Himeji answered.

"Huh? You really think so?"

"Oh, actually, I know someone. Maybe we can get them to lend us some equipment."

You know someone...? Is that what I think it is?

Himeji softly nodded upon seeing my expression.

"Really?! That's great!"

"But I can't guarantee they'll let us borrow the stuff. Let me ask first."

I figured it'd be someone she had met through her time as an idol.

She might not have been active in the industry, but it wasn't as though she'd burned any bridges.

Officially, she was only taking a break, so maybe she didn't retire entirely...?

We said good-bye and each went our own way. Once home, I plopped down on my bed.

I had to study for the makeup test, look for a job, and come up with the storyboard for the film... Crap, I had so much to do.

Yet, strangely, I didn't feel annoyed by all of it. Well, I didn't want to study for the test, that's for sure.

"Hey, Mana, where do you think I'd be able to get a part-time job?" I asked her as soon as she came home.

"You? A part-time job? Hmm... Oh, what about dishwashing?"

"At a restaurant, huh?"

"No, here at home. How's two hundred yen each time sound?"

"Look, I'm being serious..."

"Huh? I'm being serious, too?" Mana pursed her lips.

Two hundred yen for washing the dishes? What am I, a grade-schooler? It was at times like this that I was reminded of the fact that Mana was still just a middle schooler.

I was looking for jobs on my phone when I got a text from Himeji.

They said we can borrow the equipment. There are several types, so could you come to the office to check them out? I have no idea what is what.

She sure worked fast.

I wasn't an expert, either, but I couldn't just leave it up to her, so I said yes.

"Did you wait long?"

Himeji arrived at the station platform. Her street clothes gave her an entirely different look from that of her school uniform.

She was wearing a long, soft, white skirt and a sleeveless shirt. She was using a cross-body bag, which accented her chest.

I could feel my eyes wandering there, but according to Mana and Torigoe, girls could tell when you did that, so I tried my best to look away.

She was also wearing glasses.

She noticed me staring at them and said:

"Oh, these? They're fake. For fashion." She smiled as she tapped the frames.

"You look a bit like a college student."

"So are you saying I look mature?"

She blinked repeatedly, and her lips curled into a smile.

Life in Tokyo had polished her looks to an outstanding degree.

It was Saturday, and we were heading to Himeji's agency to borrow equipment for the movie.

Fushimi had thespian school, and Torigoe was reviewing the screenplay, so, although she had invited everyone, only I came.

We got on the train and made our way to the office.

"You didn't quit, did you?"

"I quit being an idol, but I am only taking a break from being a celebrity."

"Huh."

A celebrity... Which is also Fushimi's goal...

"It was during my second year of middle school that I auditioned and got into the group…"

So she had about two and a half years of experience.

On the other hand, though, this meant she most likely missed school, rarely took classes, and almost never participated in school events.

"Then I started feeling physically unwell and wanted to go back to my hometown, where you and everyone was."

"You had it hard, but you did a great job."

Himeji shook her head.

"In the end, I left. The ones doing a good job are the girls still in the group."

I didn't know much about the group, but I had a sense of just how hard she worked.

It made me think about all the idols on TV who were cute, good at singing and dancing, and talked about interesting topics… They were mostly around my age, and they were all on TV and onstage after working hard for it.

I had seen some documentary-style programs where they follow them everywhere, but even then, it didn't feel real that they were ordinary girls like her. Having it be someone you know really makes a difference.

I was also impressed that Himeji never talked in an arrogant or conceited way when the topic was brought up.

Compared to when she talked to me.

"So you said that I look like a college student in these clothes. Does that mean I look good in them? You like this sort of clothing?" She grinned mischievously and stared at me.

I stared back and noticed something different about her.

Is that makeup? Not the same she puts on all the time, at least.

"I won't say you don't look good."

"Hee-hee. Got it, Mr. Roundabout."

After an hour-and-a-half-long trip, we arrived at the station closest to the office, and Himeji lead the way there.

My eyes darted about at the sheer amount of people walking on the streets.

"Watch out, or they'll discover you're a bumpkin," she warned me.

I kept that in mind.

We arrived at a multi-tenant building where a convenience store occupied the first floor.

"This store saved me many times," Himeji said, sounding nostalgic, despite it not being so long ago.

We got on the elevator, and she pressed the LEVEL 4 button right away. The sign next to it read REIJI PA.

"The agency is called Reiji Performing Arts."

"Never heard of them."

"Figured. Most people don't know about the agency, even if they know the group."

There was an intercom right outside the elevator. Himeji picked it up and said, "Hello, it's Himejima." After a while, the door at the end of the hallway opened up.

A fashionable man in his late thirties came out and waved at us. Himeji gave a slight bow.

"Hello, Mr. Matsuda."

"Aika! How've you beeeen?" he said, extending the last word with a gentle smile.

He was good-looking even upon first glance—I thought he was a model.

"I've been well. Been healthy ever since."

"I'm sooo glad!"

Then Himeji introduced me.

"This is Mr. Matsuda. He's the director and chief manager of Reiji PA."

"N-nice to meet you… I'm Takamori."

Mr. Matsuda stared intently at me.

"You're the childhood friend Ryou? Nice eyes… So cloudy. So murky. Yum."

Is that…nice?

Wouldn't nice be clear *or* bright?

Also…"yum"?!

"Oh, he holds both positions, since the agency's so small."

No, Himeji, that's not what I'm confused about.

"Sooo you're here for camera, mic, and lights, right? Wait just a minute in the reception room, okay?"

"Will do," Himeji answered, then entered the office without hesitation and opened the door at the back.

The room was furnished with two leather sofas facing each other and had a big window.

"Mr. Matsuda helped me out a lot during my time here. He also takes care of auditions."

"I see."

"Oh, could it be you're thinking about managers and idols doing naughty things with each other? Don't worry—Mr. Matsuda's gay."

Oh. Yeah, I could've guessed.

"Thank you for waiting!"

Mr. Matsuda slammed the door open with his behind, his hands occupied with two paper bags.

"I'm sorry I couldn't get you some tea. No one's here for the weekend. You know how they've been getting all pesky about always having Saturdays and Sundays off."

"They have…?"

He sat down on the sofa across the table and, from inside the paper bags, took out three cameras, three mics, and lights for the cameras.

"You can take whichever ones you like."

"You heard him."

All the cameras were compact and weren't as heavy as I thought.

Mr. Matsuda gave me a quick rundown of the equipment.

I grabbed a camera from a famous manufacturer and tried peering through the viewfinder.

…I'm really using this to film a movie, huh.

I got chills down my spine.

"You don't need to look through that, by the way. The image appears on the display."

"Ah…"

Himeji giggled.

I had pretty much already made up my mind to grab this one ever since hearing the specs. The mics all seemed basically the same, so I chose the newest one. And I picked a small light, the easiest to work with.

"Just don't break the camera, okay? It's expensive," Himeji said.

"Hey, don't scare me like that."

Mr. Matsuda stared intently at me while I was checking out the camera.

"You've really got…such good eyes. So, so turbid."

Is that supposed to be a compliment? Am I supposed to be happy about it?

He kindly taught me how to use the equipment I'd chosen.

I was grateful for his help as it saved me the time of having to look up the details on the Internet.

I must say, even I found him to be quite handsome. He wasn't what one would call a *"hottie,"* but he was a manly sort of handsome.

"Aika, do you have some time?"

"Yes, sure. What's the matter?"

"I've gotta talk to you about something important. Sorry to interrupt your date."

"Date"…? Well, I guess it looks like that to others?

"I-it's not a date! We're just here to choose the equipment… I didn't see it that way…" She strongly denied it, red in the face.

I nodded in support like a bobblehead.

The denial had come off as too strong as Mr. Matsuda widened his eyes.

"That insistent? Ooooh... I see, I see. I understand." He glanced at me, then her, and back to me. "Good thing you quit Sakurairo Moment, huh? Couldn't have done this then."

"Mr. Matsuda! I—I didn't... I'm not here with that in mind." She denied it further, getting redder.

"But you're wearing your best clothes."

"Bwugh!" she exclaimed bizarrely. "I'm going to the restroom..." Then she escaped.

"She's cute, isn't she?"

"I've never seen her like this."

I couldn't really picture Himeji being teased that much; I wasn't expecting her to react that way.

"Himeji... Himejima's right. We're not here on a date or anything, so please don't tease her so much."

Mr. Matsuda chuckled under his breath.

I guess his laugh isn't effeminate, at least.

"She's so much more cheerful now. You should've seen her before she quit SakuMome; she looked so, so devoid of life."

"Really?"

"Yes... But I get it. She's only a girl."

Mr. Matsuda nodded repeatedly, once again deducing answers to his own questions.

"So did you *do it* yet?"

"Bwagh?!" I started choking, my saliva having gone down the wrong pipe.

"Oh my—are you all right?"

"I-I'm fine. I just wasn't expecting that weird question..."

"I was only asking, geez. You're red as a tomato."

"It's only because I was just choking. And we're not even dating, so, like…"

"I just have to know, as the director of this agency. Aika hasn't quit entirely." He smiled.

He told me the agency had multiple idol groups and that Himeji's was very successful by the company's standards.

"We weren't *that* popular," Himeji said as she came into the room; she'd managed to hear the last bit.

"Well, now that she's back, I'm sorry, Ryou, but could I ask you to leave the room?"

"I understand. I'll be outside."

I put the equipment into the paper bag and stood up.

"Wait, Ryou, you're looking for a job, right? Did you find one yet?" Himeji stopped me.

"Not yet. Why?"

"Mr. Matsuda, he's looking for a part-time job over the summer. Do you have anything for him?"

"Are you okay with working for us?" he asked me.

"I don't really know where else to go, so I would highly appreciate it."

"Hmm, let me see if we have something." He glanced upward, pensive, then said, "I'll let you know through Aika if we have anything."

I guess it was too brazen to ask for a job all of a sudden. I doubt there's much of a chance for something.

"Thank you. Please let me know if you do." I bowed, then thanked him for the equipment again and left the office.

I didn't wait for long. Himeji soon came out, and we moved to a nearby café.

Himeji said she loved the place, and I could see why. The inside was really quiet, with cozy jazz music playing in the background. I was also grateful for the fact that they didn't blast the AC like they do at convenience stores, so it wasn't ridiculously chilly inside the café.

The mature bartender brought us the omelet rice we'd ordered.

"So, what were you talking about?"

"Wanna know?" Himeji held the spoon in her mouth as she shot me a provocative glance.

"If you can't tell me, then don't. I imagine there's a reason why he had me leave the room."

Himeji exclaimed in delight at the deliciousness of the dish. She licked the demi-glace sauce from her lip.

"We talked about auditions."

"Huh?"

"Yeah, the agency was notified of an audition for the lead role in a musical. Mr. Matsuda asked if I wanted to participate. Looking for different paths from that of an idol, basically."

"So you're going to keep working in the industry?"

"You don't want me to?"

I shook my head. "You have my support."

"Thank you."

She poked my leg with her foot.

Her skinny, pale legs peeked out from under her skirt; I could see her fancy but modest pedicure, as she wore open-toe sandals.

"I feel bad for abandoning the other members of SakuMome, but I don't regret working as an idol. I was just getting interested in this line of work, so I was thinking of giving it a try. I have nothing to lose."

Nothing to lose, eh? Yeah, it's important to look at things that way.

I'm always scared of trying anything. Even about being the director for our short film—I wouldn't have done it if it weren't for Fushimi encouraging me.

"I have much to learn from you."

"Who are you and what did you do to Ryou?"

"I don't usually say that sort of thing; I get it."

We continued eating our omelets when suddenly, Himeji grimaced out of nowhere.

"I'm glad you're more positive now, but…it was Hina, wasn't it? She influenced you to change your outlook."

I didn't deny it. She pouted.

"Can't beat being by your side all the time, huh…"

I couldn't say anything and finished my lunch before her.

I glanced outside and saw the shimmer of heat haze. I looked up the weather on my phone. Temperatures were that of the peak of summer, and it would rain in the evening.

"Why not try out the camera, since you have nothing else to do?" Himeji suggested while I was waiting for her to finish eating.

"Can you not say it that way?"

I did want to try using the camera, though, so I took it out of the bag. Himeji got in the mood, too, and took off her glasses and rubbed the space between her eyes. I stared at her in confusion.

"I have to do this, or they will leave marks."

"I'm already filming, by the way."

"Wha—?! Say so sooner!" She fluttered her feet beneath the table.

"I'll delete it afterward."

"No, keep it. Make sure to keep it so you don't forget that the first thing you filmed with that camera was me."

Is that really anything important? I tilted my head.

She held her hair back with her hand as she brought the spoon to her mouth. *Maybe I can get an objective perspective of her through the display?*

First objective observation: She really was pretty.

She finished eating, and after a while, we paid for the meal and left the place.

"That was a nice café."

"I know, right?"

"The weather forecast said it'd rain, so…" I started walking toward the station, but then she grabbed my sleeve.

"C'mon, we came all the way here…" Himeji was making a more serious expression than I'd expected when I turned around. "Don't say you want to go home already."

Himeji and I walked down the street with the cries of the cicadas…or rather, the exhaust of the cars in the background.

I felt the heat even more after being inside the cool café.

"There's this place I want to go together," Himeji said, so I followed her, but I had no idea where she wanted to go.

She stopped me as I was trying to go home, but it wasn't as though I had any plans, so I decided to accompany her.

If I'd gone home, I probably would have just played around with the camera to familiarize myself with it.

"There it is. It's been a while since I came here. Have you ever been here?" Himeji pointed toward a huge shopping mall, one famous enough for me to know it. "Actually, have you ever been to Tokyo?"

"Yes?"

"Reeeally?" She grinned.

"Stop treating me like a hick."

Well, I hadn't come to Tokyo for anything other than hanging out and doing some shopping.

I didn't even understand what the difference was between the clothes in this mall and the ones you could get in our town. The only clear difference between the malls was the amount of people.

So I really had no need to visit Tokyo.

Tons of girls, both our age and around middle school age, flowed into the building, and we entered as well.

Then, all of a sudden, she locked my arm with hers.

"…Himeji."

"Yes? What could it be?"

"Your arm…"

"What's wrong with it?"

She knew exactly what I meant, but she tilted her head in feigned ignorance.

"Let me go."

"No," she refused with a smile.

Why?

The place was full of schoolgirls. I primarily saw middle and high schoolers and possibly a couple of grade-schoolers.

"We're going to the sixth floor," Himeji said as she dragged me into the elevator.

The inside of the elevator became more and more crowded (with girls, to boot), and it was packed tight by the time the doors closed.

There was no space—Himeji and I naturally ended up glued to each other. I was making sure to not touch any other girl, which inevitably led me to draw even closer to Himeji.

It felt awkward, like accidentally wandering into the women-only carriage on the train. I couldn't even look anywhere but the sign showing the floor numbers.

"Ryou," Himeji whispered.

"Hmm?"

"N-nothing…"

Himeji looked away, confused.

She seemed like she wanted to say something but couldn't. That was rare for her.

Huh?

Then I noticed that due to the lack of space and the fact that we were locking arms, my upper arm was pressed against her chest.

I could feel my face turn red.

"Ah! H-Himeji, I…"

I tried apologizing, but if I attempted to move away from her, then I would touch another girl.

"…"

Don't just stay quiet. Say something! You're only making it more awkward!

Then we finally arrived at the sixth floor. "We're getting off here," I said as I maneuvered my way through the crowd.

I pulled Himeji with me—otherwise, she would've been stuck and left behind.

"That was beyond my control, okay? Just saying."

"I—I know. You wouldn't do that on purpose. I don't mind."

Yet she wouldn't look me in the eye.

"So how does it feel to touch your childhood friend's breasts with your elbow?"

I felt her growth firsthand. Or rather, first-elbow? But I would never say that out loud.

"Don't ask me that… I did not poke anything." I sighed.

Himeji giggled.

"Yeah, I'm teasing you."

"How nice of you."

She giggled a bit more, then glanced at me with a mischievous look.

"Mine are bigger than Hina's, you know?"

…I can tell.

"What do you hope to accomplish by telling me that?"

"Nothing, I'm just stating the facts," she said rhythmically.

We walked through the mall, unconsciously holding hands.

She finally stopped before an apparel shop. The mannequins in front were wearing colorful swimsuits, in line with the season.

"Well then, let's go."

"You want me to go inside?! Gimme a break!"

"We're here to buy a swimsuit. I was thinking of giving you the right to choose mine."

I don't want that right.

I pointed at the bench across from the store.

"I'll wait here. You go buy it."

"You only have trouble coming in because your mind is full of dirty thoughts." She tapped the half-naked mannequin. "Are you getting horny looking at these mannequins wearing bikinis?"

"I am not."

"Then what's the problem?"

I guess…nothing? I don't get it anymore.

I couldn't argue back, and she dragged me into the store.

She headed straight to the swimsuit corner. I narrowed my eyes so as to see the least I possibly could.

Won't the clerks give me weird looks? I feel their eyes on me…

"Ha-ha-ha! What's with that face?"

"It's just my face."

Don't laugh at my noble attempt to avoid embarrassment.

Or, wait, are the clerks giving me weird looks because I'm making a funny face?

Himeji ignored my sense of shame and looked for her swimsuit.

"What about this one?" She grabbed a bathing suit and placed it in front of her body.

"It looks nice."

"So you like this design."

"Not really…"

"What about this one?"

"Suits you."

"I see… So I look good in everything." Himeji sighed and shook her head. "My stylist always praised that about me, said all outfits look good on me."

Are you bragging?

I supposed her confidence came from the fact that it had been a professional complimenting her. No wonder she was overconfident.

"What about this?"

"Looks good."

"Do you even mean it?" She narrowed her eyes.

"I do."

I just don't know which one would be better.

Himeji took my words at face value and called out to a clerk to let her use the fitting room, taking all three bathing suits with her.

A sigh escaped my mouth.

I didn't want any of the other female customers to stare at me, so I decided to leave the store. I figured she'd just buy whichever of the three she liked most and be done with it.

I was sitting on the bench outside when the clerk who had been giving me weird looks came out of the store and walked toward me.

"Your girlfriend wants you to see the swimsuit. Would you mind coming?"

"Wha—?" I blinked a couple of times.

I didn't even know where to begin…

She beckoned me with her hand, and I reentered the store.

She took me to the dressing room at the back and said, "Take your time!" with that trademark high-pitched voice and left with a smile.

Himeji poked her head out from behind the curtain.

"I'm wearing it."

"Himeji, please…"

She slid open the curtain before I could complain.

Her pale skin shone under the lighting, accentuating her shapely collarbone. Just as she said, her breasts were fuller than Fushimi's. The swimsuit, decorated with black ribbons, contrasted beautifully with her skin.

She was too close—I couldn't look directly at her. I could only glance sideways.

"I-it looks good."

"Honestly, I think this one looks the best, though I feel it may be a bit too mature looking."

She spun around. The ribbons on the sides of her hips bounced, as did her breasts once she stopped.

"Want to take a look at the others, too?"

"N-no. I-it's fine. Don't."

"Aw."

"Aren't you embarrassed, Himeji? About, you know, showing it to me. A man."

"Um, well, I was self-conscious at first, but I'm already used to it."

Oh, right. My childhood friend's a former idol. Of course she'd wear swimsuits for work... Wait, she did?

"The others should look good on me, too."

"Okay..."

"In fact, since everything looks good on me, I can be whatever kind of girl you like."

Himeji paid for the swimsuit and came out of the store. She definitely didn't need me for that, so I received no further complaints for waiting outside.

We bought ice cream at the food court on the first floor. I took a bite using the tiny plastic spoon.

"Why did you want a swimsuit?"

The food court was packed. Himeji ate her own ice cream—same store, different flavor.

"Why? Don't you remember that one scene?"

"What scene?"

"Aren't we filming at the sea for our movie?"

I tapped my knee.

Right. There was a scene at the beach. Though I was pretty sure she didn't need a swimsuit for it.

"You don't have to wear one, though."

Himeji heaved a heavy sigh and shook her head.

"It's not for filming. Surely, we'll be taking some breaks then play around on the beach afterward."

"No, we're going straight home."

"You misanthropic... We're high schoolers! It's the summer! How can we go to the beach and not have fun?!"

I tilted my head in confusion.

It's too hot, and the sand is coarse and rough and irritating. To be honest, I don't have many fond memories of the beach.

"My last school didn't have swimming classes, so I needed a bathing suit. The one from middle school...well...it doesn't fit."

We didn't have swimming lessons at our school, either.

I figured Fushimi could still fit in her middle school swimsuit, at least.

"And I'm sure Hina will also get herself a new one, since I got one, too."

I guess Torigoe is doing the same as well, then? She might've guessed that we'd be playing at the beach when she wrote that scene, so she would know if she needed one.

"Can I have a bite of your ice cream? I'll give you one of mine."

I had vanilla ice cream. Himeji had strawberry. I scooped a bit and held the spoon out to her.

She leaned forward and licked it off.

"Vanilla's not bad," she said before scooping a bite of her own ice cream. "Here you go."

"Um..."

"It's gonna melt—hurry, hurry," she said rhythmically.

I looked around, feeling self-conscious, and found a couple doing the same thing.

"Why are you worried? You're only making it awkward."

"I-I'm not..."

She was right.

Seeing others doing it, too, I plucked up the courage and ate it. The slightly sweet taste of strawberry spread throughout my mouth.

"Yummy, isn't it?"

"Yeash," I replied with a weird combination of sounds.

Himeji touched her lips with her finger.

"Now we've kissed."

"I-indirectly, maybe. And...you basically forced me into it. Threatened me, saying it was gonna melt soon..."

"Ah-ha-ha," she laughed. "No need to get so flustered. Geez, it's like you're a middle schooler."

"Shut it..."

"Girls share things with each other like this all the time. Boys don't?"

"No."

I didn't know for sure, though. I didn't really hang out with other guys since I got into high school.

Just as we finished our desserts, Himeji said:

"I'm used to these things because of my job, but I wouldn't show myself in a swimsuit or share my ice cream with someone I didn't like."

"Uh, thanks, I guess...?"

I didn't know how else to respond; I didn't get what she was hinting at.

As there was nothing else she wanted to do at the mall, we decided to leave, and just as we were exiting the building, I felt a drop of water on my head.

I looked up and saw the sky covered in dark clouds. Rain was just starting to fall.

"It's raining..."

I was about to say we should hurry to the station when it started pouring.

"We should take shelter somewhere."

"...Right."

Then a strong white light flashed, followed by a booming sound.

"Eek!"

Lightning must have struck nearby. I tucked my head in out of reflex. Himeji was also scared—she was clinging to me.

"Sorry... I can't handle thunder."

"So that part of you hasn't changed."

"L-let's go."

Before I could ask where, she pointed at a nearby karaoke bar. That was the closest place where we could take shelter from the rain.

The rain kept on getting heavier. We had no time to think of other spots.

"Okay, let's go."

Himeji kept clinging to me as we hurried to the karaoke bar.

We registered at the reception area and went to our assigned room. Whether it was because nothing else was available or because there were only two of us, it was a tiny room.

Only the light from the TV screen illuminated the dark space.

"Here we won't have to hear the thunder, either. Pretty good choice, if I do say so myself," Himeji said as she took out a hand towel from her bag and used it to dry her hair and clothes.

"Here, use this."

She handed me a handkerchief, but I declined.

"It'll dry soon enough."

Handkerchief and *hand towel. She sure is well prepared, huh.*

"Since we're here now, how about we sing some songs?"

"Nah, I'm a terrible singer," I said.

"Then this is a good opportunity for you to practice."

"What?"

"You see, you'll never get good at singing if you don't practice. It's like sports."

I guess?

She was a professional in the field—I had no reason to doubt her.

I grabbed the tablet to look for a song, while Himeji peered at the screen from beside me, keeping a hand on my knee.

"Something easy, something easy..."

I chose a couple of songs I knew and started singing.

"You're not bad, actually," she said, blinking in amazement. "Okay, now choose one for me. Anything you want, I'll do it."

What a pro.

What should I choose, though...?

I kept browsing, undecided, until I thought of one and slowly inputted the words.

Oh...there we go.

"Moment" by Sakurairo Moment.

"This one, then." I pushed the button, and the tablet beeped.

"Huh?" She groaned as soon as she saw the title on the screen.

"You said 'anything.'"

"V-very well. I'll go all out. I'll even dance, too."

She steeled herself.

"You don't need to go that far."

"You don't know me as an idol, do you, Ryou? It's time you did. Take a good look."

She exhaled like an Olympic athlete. She took off her glasses and put them on the table.

"Yell *hey* when I give you the signal during the chorus."

"Huh? Wha—?"

"You chose this, so we're going to do it right."

It seemed I got her weirdly fired up.

Her eyes were serious.

We moved the table to a corner so it wouldn't get in the way. The intro started playing, and she hopped and grabbed at the air.

I'd never heard this song, but I immediately liked it—the up-tempo tune was exhilarating.

Himeji's singing was great, obviously.

She blushed a bit when our eyes met, but she continued on.

I figured it was all part of the act. She smiled and winked a few times just at the right moments, then kept on singing.

I wasn't really interested in idols and had never been to a concert, but I felt I understood how the fans would feel at one.

I could understand why Shinohara loved Aika so much.

"H-hey!" I exclaimed as she signaled, but she beckoned me to put more energy into it.

I started getting the timing right after a few times.

"Hey!!"

"Not there!"

I felt my face turn red at the rebuke.

Himeji giggled upon finishing the song. She had this look of fulfillment as she caught her breath.

"That was the first time I ever went all out in front of one person."

"You did great. You looked cute."

"Wha—?!"

For the first time ever, I understood how concertgoers felt.

I nodded repeatedly in understanding, while Himeji became flustered.

"Huh? Uh…? I-i-it would've been better with the right outfit, but, um… D-don't just praise me like that all of a sudden!"

She hit me softly.

Why am I getting yelled at for complimenting her?

◆Hina Fushimi◆

I went back to my room after taking a bath and noticed Ryou had already sent me the filming schedule.

"Wha…?! The beach?"

Was there such a scene? I flipped through Shii's script and found it. We definitely had to film at the beach. Even the dialogue mentioned it, so she must've really wanted to go to one if she included it in the movie.

The schedule itself wasn't very detailed, but it took note of all the important points: it was just like Ryou to do that.

"Good job!"

I lay down on my bed and merrily fluttered my feet.

We're going to the beach! I can't wait.

I felt like I could function for three days just on the energy this was giving me.

Wait a second… We're going to the beach…

"Which means…I need a swimsuit… I can't use the same one from middle school! I need a new one!"

My instinct told me it would be the wrong choice if I didn't.

I had only my school swimsuit—you know, like the typical blue one with your name written on the chest.

I checked my wallet—it was empty. *Darn it, I shouldn't have bought that novel and Blu-ray!*

"D-Daaad!" I hurried downstairs.

After much begging, I successfully obtained a five-thousand-yen bill.

As I expected, he told me to just use the one from middle school. Trying to explain a girl's heart to a middle-aged man sure was exhausting. He didn't seem entirely convinced, but in the end, he gave me the money.

"Will this be enough, though…?"

I searched online and found more than enough cute swimsuits within my budget.

I began to type my response to Ryou but then stopped.

"No, he must be thinking I'd bring my middle school one. Let's surprise him."

I deleted the text saying, I wanna go buy a swimsuit. Come with me!

Right then, I got a message from Shii.

Are you bringing a swimsuit to the beach?

For sure!

Just like me, she must have been worried about having nothing besides her school swimsuit.

Wanna go get one together? I've never bought one for myself; I dunno what'd be good.

I immediately jumped on board.

Yeah! Let's go!

Let's go with Takamori's sister, too.

Mana? I tilted my head, but I had no reason to say no.

We made a group chat for the three of us and settled on a date.

We all just happened to be free the next day around noon.

I invited Ai, too, but she turned me down, saying she already had one.

I was meeting Mana at the nearby station. She was already there when I arrived.

"Oh my…" Mana closed her eyes, as though she had a headache. "I've gotten used to this already, but it's still as shocking every time."

"What is?"

"I'm glad I brought a change of clothes. Here. Put this on instead." She handed me a paper bag. "I'm not letting you go to Hamaya in that."

Hamaya was the biggest shopping district in the area. Middle and high schoolers around here mostly went there to go on dates and for shopping.

"Is it that bad?" I tilted my head.

Mana had on a sad, heartbroken expression.

"It's terrible."

Oof…

That hurt.

"Dreadful."

You can stop now.

"Hurry—we'll be late meeting up with Shizu," she urged.

Why must she be so blunt? I grumbled as I changed into the clothes Mana gave me in the restroom.

It was a minidress with a big ribbon around the navel area.

There was also a pair of sandals that completed the outfit, so I changed into those, too, before leaving the restroom.

"Now we're talking! I'm an absolute genius!"

"Mana, are you sure my underwear won't show in this? It's too short."

"You're fine. The dress is supposed to be cute and sexy like that."

Sexy…

Right, I'm already in my second year of high school. I can wear this sort of thing.

I felt my self-confidence rise.

We were meeting Shii at Hamaya Station and arrived five minutes late, as it took a while to change my clothes.

"Sorry for making you wait!"

"Whoa! The Boss is here, too!"

Yup, Shinohara was there.

We waved at them, and they responded in kind.

"She said she wanted to come, so I said, *'why not?'*" Shii explained.

I felt reassured by Shinohara's presence, though I didn't know why. Maybe because she had the aura of someone who could provide emotional support, and that's probably why Mana called her the Boss.

It felt nice, the four of us hanging out together.

After a short round of greetings, we walked toward the mall Ryou and I had visited once before.

"There's this store on the second floor that sells nice stuff at really good prices."

We got on the escalators and headed to the shop.

Since it was Mana who recommended the place, I expected it to mainly sell *gyaru*-style clothing, but although they did have some of that stuff, there was also a large variety of other neater or more casual pieces.

I grabbed the first swimsuit that caught my eye and held it up to my neck as I asked Shii for her thoughts.

"Heh, that's too gaudy."

"Huh? You think?"

"Hina, I think you'd look best in a school swimsuit…"

No, Mana. What's the point in coming here, then?

"Fushimi, I think one-pieces would suit you best," Shinohara said.

"Really? Aren't they too childish?"

Mana checked out some of the designs and grabbed one to show me.

"This one doesn't look childish at all."

"Hmm. Hmm, hmm, hmmmm."

"Hiina's turning into an owl."

The swimsuit exposed the shoulders and back, so it really didn't look like a one-piece at first glance.

"I could even walk around the streets in this!"

All three gave me weird looks.

"No, Hina. This is a swimsuit."

"Huh? I…I was just kidding."

I was honestly confused. They all sighed in relief.

They then proceeded to look for their own bathing suits.

They were all such nice friends.

I talked about the designs with Shinohara while Shii and Mana chatted about something else.

"Sis."

"Yes, Shizu?"

"Wanna be our stylist and hairdresser?"

"Hmm?"

"For our movie. I mentioned it before, remember? I think you'd be perfect."

"Really? Are you okay with me? Shouldn't it be one of your classmates?"

Mana noticed Shinohara and I were listening in, and she pointed at herself and looked at us as she said that.

"I think you'd be great!" I gave her a thumbs-up. "Ryou didn't even think about that position. I also thought we would be fine without one, since it shouldn't be too complicated."

Thinking about it now, though, you always saw the stylists' names in the credits of any movie.

"See? And you're very good at dressing people up. So I think you'd do great," Shinohara said while looking at the swimsuits.

"If you say so, Boss. Maybe I'll give it a try."

"How many times have I told you to stop calling me that?"

"Sorry, sorry. Don't get mad." Mana giggled. "I'll ask Bubby. If he says it's okay, I'll do it."

That was it, then. We had a stylist and hairdresser. Besides, Ryou had no reason to say no.

"I mean, you do have someone who's tough to handle, with whom I have experience."

Why's she looking at me?

The conversation soon turned back to discussing the swimsuits. I asked Mana for her opinions, then the clerk, and after much deliberation, I decided to buy the one-piece.

I was hoping to get a bikini, but Mana and the clerk cleverly guided me away from that whenever I brought it up.

"What did you buy, Shii?" I asked her on the way home.

"I…just got a normal one."

"What's it like?"

"I-it's nothing amazing… I'll be wearing a jacket on top anyway."

She's flustered. How cute.

"I think you were right to follow Mana's and the store clerk's recommendation, by the way," she said.

"You think? Why?"

"'Cause you don't really have a chest."

"But I do?"

"We can't have your top slipping off with the slightest motion. There's nothing to keep it in place."

"There is! And I'd stuff it!"

"This isn't a tooth cavity we're talking about here."

That got a chuckle out of me. "What?" I started laughing.

Shii also laughed with me.

"I've always wanted to go to the beach with friends," she said.

"Me too. Is that why you included that scene?"

"Not really, but maybe it was part of the reason. And haven't you been there with Takamori?"

"A looong time ago. Sooo long ago."

Does he even remember?

We parted ways with Shinohara and Shii at the station, and Mana and I took the next train home.

I had to give back her clothes, so I stopped by the Takamori house.

"I'm home, Bubby!" Mana shouted as soon as we arrived, loud enough so he'd hear from upstairs.

"Yeah, yeah, welcome back. And I told you to stop calling me that..."

I heard the soft steps of his slippers as he came down the stairs with an irritated expression.

"Hi, Ryou."

"You're here, too?"

"I have to give these clothes back."

"Oh..." He seemed to have grasped the situation right away.

"Have you been studying for your makeup test?"

"Yes, thank you. Though it's gonna be the same exact content and questions anyway, so I could just memorize the answers."

"That's not the point of math!"

"Whatever. The point is avoiding remedial classes. Anyway. Have fun."
He waved as he walked to the living room.

I went to Mana's room upstairs.

"Why?!" she shouted as soon as I took off the dress.

"Why what?"

"Why are you wearing the swimsuit you just bought?"

"Because...I didn't want my underwear showing."

"And you don't find the swimsuit showing to be embarrassing?"

"No."

I could easily forget I was wearing a shorter skirt than usual and let my guard down; I knew myself.

"C'mon, what's so bad about showing a little? ☆"

"Never."

Mana started laughing; she knew I'd say that.

I had put my outfit from earlier in the day inside the paper bag, so I took it out piece by piece, when...

"Huh?"

"What's up, Hina?"

"...My underwear's not here."

Mana's eyes shone sharply.

"No way... You came here without wearing any undergarments?"

"Of course not!"

"So you're the kind of girl to leave her panties behind at the baths during a field trip?"

"Wha—? What're you implying?"

"You left them at the store!"

I curled up in a ball and covered my surely flushed face.

N-no way...! I totally did that...!

"Gooosh! It's your fault for giving me this exhibitionist dressss!"

"Huh? Why me? It's your fault for being such a scatterbrain!"

The clerk must be in a panic thinking someone left the store pantyless and braless.

"Wh-wh-what if they think I stole it?!"

"Did you...pay for it...while wearing it?"

"No, I just went back to the dressing room afterward, since you all weren't done yet..."

"Hey! What's the commotion?" Ryou asked from beyond the door.

"Bubby, you gotta hear this!"

"Mana, hold on!"

I'm still wearing the swimsuit!

Mana opened the door.

"What's with all the fu...?"

My eyes met Ryou's, and I immediately felt my face turn red.

"Why'd you open the door, moron?!" He looked away and slammed the door shut.

He saw... I wanted him to see it at the beach... It was supposed to be a surprise...

"Ahhh... It's over..."

"It's a swimsuit! What's the harm?!"

"That's not the issue…"

She couldn't bear the sight of me sitting on the floor and hugging my knees, and she called the store.

"They found them. A lost bra and pair of panties." She grinned at her own words. "Who loses her own underwear?"

"Did you tell them I didn't steal anything?"

"I didn't. Just take the receipt with you, and it'll be okay."

How am I supposed to go back to that store now, though…? I'm going to die out of sheer embarrassment…

"Hina, as ancient philosophers first said…"

"Yes?"

"Don't sweat it."

"Yeah… Thanks…"

"Y-you look dead inside… I've never seen you like this."

I went back to the store, wearing Mana's dress and the swimsuit underneath.

I don't even remember how many times I apologized, but the clerk just kept smiling, as she said she was glad they found their way back to their owner.

…They must think I left this store without any underwear… I mean… technically, they're not wrong…

I blocked out my emotions as I thought about it.

I passed the makeup test without any issues. It was two days before the last day of school that I was told I'd be able to have a summer break free of remedial classes.

Mana volunteered to be the movie's stylist, and I accepted on the spot.

I was worried at first, since she had her high school entrance exams this year, but it's Mana we're talking about. I had never heard of her having bad grades, so it probably wasn't an issue.

I was drawing a rough storyboard for Torigoe's screenplay when someone suddenly pulled back the chair in front, then placed their elbow on my desk and rested their head on their hand.

I looked up. It was Deguchi.

"Need anything?"

"C'mon, Takayan. We're friends."

We had become close during the school field trip—he was, probably, the only classmate I could really call my friend.

"Anything I can help with?"

"You already have a very important job…as a background character."

"Clearly not if I'm in the background!" He immediately pointed out the contradiction.

Deguchi was Classmate L for the classroom scenes. Background characters were assigned a letter, alphabetically, starting from A.

"Whatever. I mean, I wanna help with the filming. You'll need help, right?"

"Well… I wouldn't know until we actually start."

Deguchi pointed his thumb at his chest. "C'mon. This is what friends are for."

He had this awkward smile as I glanced back down at my desk.

"You don't get embarrassed saying that?"

"Shut your trap."

He cleared his throat before putting on a serious face.

"Okay, I'll cut to the chase."

You were just buttering me up?

"I really want to help with filming. Please, I'll do anything. I'll even carry the bags if that's all there is."

"You find that fun or what?"

"It's not fair only you get to spend the summer with the two prettiest girls in our class, nay, the entire school."

So herein lay your true intentions.

He must've been referring to Fushimi and Himeji.

When I think about it, the crew was all girls except for me. But half of the group were my childhood friends, and my sister was with us, so I didn't really mind it. But I suppose having another guy with me would be nice.

"Okay, how about you act as my megaphone?"

"Whatcha mean?"

"You know how they yell, *Three, two, one, action?* Or, *cut?* Stuff like that."

"Hey, that's the director's main job!"

"It is not." *What do you take directors for?* "I could just say it myself, but your voice is louder, right? I think it's the perfect job for you."

"Yes, yes, yes, yes!"

Deguchi drew his face close to mine, all excited. I pushed it away.

"Cool. Okay then, I'll text you the schedule later."

"Awesome!"

He's actually cool with it, huh.

I hadn't really spoken to him since the field trip, but I was looking forward to hanging out with him again.

I spent the following two days in relative peace, reading manga and watching movies to use as reference for our project.

Sometimes I took notes and wrote down ideas for the composition directly on the screenplay. Things like, Let's do it like they did in xyz. Maybe you could say that I was just copying them, but hey, I was still learning. Please understand.

Then came the last day of school. Classes ended before noon, and we were on the chilly, air-conditioned train on our way back home.

Fushimi was looking at the screenplay. Her own copy was full of notes, and though it's only been a week, it was already all worn out.

She had asked me a lot about her acting, like how she should perform in certain scenes.

"It's finally tomorrow."

"Too bad we still have to go to school even though it's summer break."

"I'm nervous about it but also very excited."

Same.

I had already learned how to handle the equipment we borrowed, so I was hoping we wouldn't run into trouble during the actual filming.

"Hina, is this afternoon okay?" Himeji asked her.

"Yeah, sure. Let's, please."

"Huh? Okay for what?" I asked.

"You don't need to know," Himeji replied.

"A read-through. Ai said she wanted to rehearse together." Fushimi immediately spilled the beans.

"I said he didn't need to know…"

"Why not? Let him know that you're putting in the effort."

Oh, I see… Himeji, you're the kind of person to study real hard before an exam and then say you've done nothing at all, aren't you?

"We've already practiced a few times, actually."

"Wow."

I glanced at Himeji in surprise, and she looked away with awkward resentment.

I had figured she would leave it all up to luck at the crucial moment, considering how high her self-esteem was. So I didn't expect her to actually practice.

"Good for you."

"Don't try and compliment me if you don't know what to say." She pouted. Then muttered, "Now I can't surprise him."

Yeah, I totally would've been shocked, after seeing how terrible she did when they competed for the main role... The disappointment on her face was tremendous.

I was reminded of how everyone was working to the best of their abilities for each of their roles. I never thought about half-assing my job, but now I was even more motivated to put my all into filming.

It had been a long journey since we decided to make a movie, but the first day of filming finally came.

The travel bag was bulging with makeup tools, and the suitcase was rattling with an excess of outfits. "Outfits" that were all from Mana's own closet. If you were to describe the clothes she wore at home as her "farm team," then the ones in this suitcase would be the "starting lineup."

"Do we really need that much?"

"I mean, better safe than sorry. We're not coming back all the way home if it turns out we need something extra."

Mana and I were on our way to school, our shooting location, alongside our two childhood friends.

Fushimi, Himeji, and I were wearing our school uniforms, but Mana was in her casual clothes, which made her stand out even more than usual.

I already told you which scenes we're shooting today. You should know what clothes we need. And that's our uniform. It takes place at school.

After a few minutes of walking from the station, we soon saw the school building.

I could see Mana failing to hold back her giggling.

"I'm so excited to see your school."

"You're taking the entrance exams soon, right, Mana? Have you decided which high school to apply to?" Himeji asked.

Mana shook her head. "Nope."

"Come to our school!" Fushimi said.

"I'll think about it."

Huh. Maybe she wants to go elsewhere?

Mana followed anxiously behind us as we entered the school grounds and headed to our classroom.

It was ten minutes before our meeting time. I wondered if the others had already arrived.

I peered inside and saw our ten classmates were already there. Torigoe and Deguchi, too.

We were just having them walk through the hallways, acting as the friends of the leads and such. We needed them for only this scene, but we would eventually need to have them all together, including Waka, for another one that took place in the middle of class. Only I remained behind the camera.

"Good morning!" Fushimi beamed as always as she entered the classroom.

"Good morning," Himeji said as well.

Some replied with similar greetings; then Mana and I entered. Commotion ensued.

"A *gyaru*!"

"Which school is she from?"

"She's so cute…"

I quickly introduced Mana.

"She will be our stylist and hairdresser. My sister, Mana."

Mana bowed, wearing a stiff expression. "N-ni-nice to meet you…"

Where did all the excitement go?

I explained the scene to everyone else while Mana did Fushimi's and Himeji's makeup in another room. Those two didn't usually put too much effort into it, so having Mana supervise was of great help.

I glanced at Torigoe to make sure I wasn't missing anything before I ended the explanation. Then Deguchi raised his hand.

"Director!"

"What?"

"I request more screen time for Classmate L."

"Background Character L does not appear in this scene. It's not in the script."

"Don't change his name! It's even worse now!"

He wanted a scene with Fushimi or Himeji, but if I started fulfilling each person's requests, there'd be no end to it...

He kept on arguing, and I was wavering when Torigoe spoke up.

"Background Character L, you're getting in the way of filming. Shut up." It was over for him. "I'm...sorry, but we made every decision in the story for a reason. Okay?"

"It's fine; it's fine." He waved his hand. "I should be thanking you now, actually. To think I'd get to see both your hot and cold sides in the span of a second..."

Deguchi, you are just unbelievable.

I felt bad for having Torigoe step in when it should've been my job.

Thanks, Torigoe. I'll take care of the future complaints. It is my job as director so you don't have to take the brunt of it.

"I'm sure you will all have your own opinions on how we should be making the film, but I want to let you know right now that we won't necessarily adopt all your ideas," I said. A bit late, but I had to.

Deguchi stood up from his desk and went outside, probably to take a look at the two main leads, when I heard him shout in wonder.

"Wowww! You did amazing, Mana-banana!"

"I know, right?! Praise me more!"

Everyone in the classroom turned to look at the door upon hearing the conversation. It soon opened again.

"Please welcome our main character, Hirono Shibahara, played by Miss Fushimi!" Deguchi announced before her entrance.

"Greetings!"

Fushimi usually didn't wear makeup, or if she did, it was really subtle… so now that Mana had done her makeup, her eyes looked so much bigger.

It felt like they were shining even more.

She had this greatly motivated expression.

"Now welcome Eri Akiyama, played by Miss Himejima!"

"Greetings!"

Himeji entered with dashing poise. She, too, had her…glow? aura?… super enhanced by Mana's makeup—it was dazzling.

Himeji's expression was totally natural, though. She was clearly more used to being around cameras than any of us.

It also seemed like Mana had taken the personalities of each character into account. I wasn't quite sure, but their makeup seemed distinctly fitting for each of them.

It really felt like they were Hirono Shibahara and Eri Akiyama in the flesh.

Mana, you're amazing. I'll treat you to something later.

I explained how we were gonna do the first take, then realized: Everyone…looked pretty nervous ever since the two had entered the classroom.

They must have been overwhelmed by the girls' powerful presences. They did feel like two bundles of condensed energy, full of motivation and spirit. Particularly Fushimi, being the one who'd proposed this idea in the first place and the one most experienced in acting.

I could feel the weight of responsibility on my shoulders, as the purported backbone of this project.

"I'm sure we'll have slipups in the first few takes, so let's take it easy. It's also my first time filming, so…don't worry about making mistakes," I said.

Fushimi nodded. "Yeah! Let's do this!"

Geez, keep that enthusiasm in check. Your eyes are popping out of your head. Are you looking to murder someone or what?

Himeji chuckled. "Hina, is this your first time being filmed?"

"So what?"

"Let me give you a piece of advice." She had on a smile as she placed a hand on Fushimi's shoulder. "Take it easy, rookie."

And you stop trying to get the upper hand.

"Himeji, enough of your advice; you'll only confuse everyone more."

"Okay!"

I forgot these two always compete at everything.

Their characters were like that, too. The casting was practically perfect.

I could feel there was a long road ahead of us. Things likely weren't going to go smoothly…

By the time we had to wrap up, we hadn't filmed even half of the shots we'd planned.

There were many problems: Fushimi and Himeji butted heads over every single thing, Fushimi insisted on retakes even when I gave the okay, some classmates fumbled their lines, Deguchi kept improvising, and I, too, screwed up the shots a couple of times…

It was our first day, after all, so mistakes and time wasted were bound to happen.

Himeji's acting had improved quite a lot since the last time I'd seen it; practice with Fushimi must've helped a lot. At the very least, she wasn't reading lines in a monotone this time around.

Everyone was tired after filming, even with a lunch break, and the location was about to change due to the time of day, so we decided to end it before sunset.

"Bubby, will you really make it on time?" Mana was putting on her apron as she came into the living room where I was checking what we had filmed.

"Yes... Hopefully..."

"You don't sound too sure."

"Oh, Mana, by the way, you did great on the makeup."

"'Course I did!" She smiled bashfully before going back to the kitchen.

I always saw her reading fashion magazines—maybe she was thinking about pursuing that sort of career.

Then my phone started vibrating loudly on the table. At first I thought it was a text, so I ignored it, but it kept on vibrating. I glanced at it and saw it was a call from Himeji.

"Hey, what's up?"

"Good job today."

"Oh. Sure. You too. Practice served you well. Nice acting."

"Seriously?!"

"Seriously."

"I'm glad you've taken notice of my potential." I could picture her smug expression. *"But anyway, I'm calling about the job with Mr. Matsuda."*

"Whoa, really?"

I had honestly thought it would end up going nowhere.

"Are you still looking for one?"

"Yeah, I'm still searching."

"Good. Mr. Matsuda said he wants you to come to the office tomorrow at one PM."

"Gotcha. What's the job about?"

"He just said he wants your help with something."

Help with...what?

Even without any details, I couldn't just turn this opportunity down.

"I'm Takamori," I said into the intercom, just as Himeji had done the last time. "I'm here for the job offer from Mr. Matsuda...your chief manager."

"Just one moment, please," the woman on the other end said before hanging up.

After about five minutes, Mr. Matsuda came out of his office.

"Ryou, good to see you!"

"Thank you for having me."

Going right for "Ryou," huh. Only girls I know really well call me that... Feels weird to have him do it.

"I heard I would be helping you with something?"

"Yes, that's right."

The pay was eight thousand yen per day, which was a whole lot of money. What was he gonna make me do...?

Mr. Matsuda beckoned me to come in, noticing my anxiety.

I followed him to his office, and in a corner of the room, there was a small desk, a chair, and a laptop. They all looked haphazardly placed.

Mr. Matsuda opened the laptop and turned it on.

"Ryou, are you good with computers?"

"I'm average, I guess."

"I'm terrible with these things, and all the office staff is busy with other work, so I needed some help."

"I see..."

He wanted me to contact various people through email and texts.

I guessed I worried for nothing. I could do that.

"We had someone doing this job, but they quit last month. I thought we could go on without hiring someone new, but no. It's been difficult, and the work is piling up." He shook his head with a troubled smile.

Apparently, my talk about searching for a job turned out to be a lifesaver.

My main job was to check any emails we received, tell Mr. Matsuda what they said, then write a reply.

"I'll be doing my own work over here," he said before sitting at his own desk, grabbing a pen and paper and writing something down.

I did as instructed and opened the emails, conveyed their contents, and typed up the responses, time and again.

"…Wait. Uh-oh. Ryou, are you writing proper business emails? I mean, I had this idea that the young'uns only knew how to type in their newfangled texting styles."

"You are not entirely wrong. I have no real knowledge of how to write proper business emails, but I'm copy-pasting what the previous employee wrote, then changing the details to match."

"Choppy-pasta? Um, okay, it sounds like you're doing well, then? That's good."

He doesn't know what copy-pasting is?

"Yes. Though could you check it before I send it, please?"

This one was for a client, so I had to make sure I wasn't being rude or anything. I was writing them to the best of my knowledge, but I didn't know much about proper etiquette regarding business emails.

If it happened that the previous employee had made a mistake, then I'd just be making the same ones.

I carried the laptop to his desk and turned the screen toward him.

"Hmm… Oh my, you're such a capable man… My heart flutters."

Please don't.

I went back to my desk. As I kept on working, I became comfortable enough to make some small talk in the middle of work.

"Was Himeji really feeling so unwell before quitting?"

"She really was. We talked about what to do next, about what she wanted to do this time around. She wasn't in the right headspace for that last time."

That bad? I can't picture her like that.

"She was super down at the time…but now she's back to being the Aika I know well. I think that's thanks to you, Ryou."

"I didn't do anything."

"I think it's what she needed. Even though it's a lesser-known group, she was still pretty popular; some say it was a waste for her to leave, but I think it was for the best."

"She was that popular?"

"You didn't know?" He seemed taken aback.

He rummaged through his desk's drawers and took out a DVD. Written in marker was *Sakurairo Moment Concert* along with a date on the cover.

"You can have this."

"Thank you," I said as I took the DVD from his hand.

Himeji's idol era was documented on this disc.

I had already heard her sing live at karaoke, but she did say, *"That wasn't the full extent of my skill, just so you know."*

"She said she was interested in acting; I don't know why," Mr. Matsuda said.

"Acting, eh?"

"But I can conjure up a reason. Not that I can completely see through her, but this was pretty obvious."

"Are you talking about the audition?"

"Did she tell you?"

"Yes. The look on her face as she told me she'd be rising up to the challenge was quite reassuring."

"I see. I'm glad to hear she's back in form."

Mr. Matsuda stared into space, as though reminiscing.

He must have been very worried about Himeji.

"There's no choice…"

I couldn't hear everything he whispered. I glanced at him, and he shook his head with an awkward smile.

"I said, there's no choice but to take that first step if you want someone to look your way."

I helped Mr. Matsuda out a few times more after that. Since it wasn't a full-time job, and I wasn't getting paid by the hour, he always paid me out of his pocket at the end of each day.

I guessed he was probably paying me that much due to our mutual acquaintance. I started at one PM and was usually there until nighttime.

I was able to buy a used PC soon enough thanks to this job.

"Is there something you want to buy?" Mr. Matsuda asked me a few days into the job.

"I want a computer."

"If you don't mind a used one, you could take the one in the office we're not using."

Honestly, I nearly gave in. But I turned down the offer. Not knowing much about specs was one thing, but I started this job to buy myself a computer in the first place.

"That's quite admirable, young man," he said.

The one I bought felt like a very advanced toy that was hard to handle.

I transferred the clips we shot to the editing software I'd also bought and started playing around with it.

We had asked our classmates who had their own band or played the piano to produce four tracks for the film. I could just put the music in after editing the rest, so that part could wait until after summer break.

At first, we were going to use copyright-free music, but Fushimi didn't want that. She said it felt cheap, and since we had classmates who could take care of it, we should ask them.

I figured the latter was the main reason. It was something only Fushimi could plan, since she knew the interests and skills of our whole class.

Everyone helped in all sorts of ways—acting as minor characters, helping out with finer details in filming, music, etc. Everyone had done something already by this point, but the film was still far from being complete.

"Oh, you're still at it!" Mana opened the door to my room just as I was staring at the monitor on my desk.

"What do you want?"

"We gotta get up early tomorrow, Bubby. You better not oversleep like the other day. I'm gonna slap you to death if you do."

I glanced at the clock on the screen. It was already past midnight.

"That late already?" It was only then that I remembered we had to get up early the next day to go to the beach. "We should've gone to the nearest beach."

That had been my idea in the first place, but the filming crew, mainly Fushimi and Torigoe, had strongly refused.

"We should take the opportunity to go somewhere farther!" Fushimi had said, and Torigoe agreed, much to my surprise.

I didn't know what the point of doing that was, but then Deguchi and Mana also agreed, so I ended up in the minority.

"What about you, Mana? What're you doing up so late?"

"I was preparing food, duh!"

We're bringing our own food?

"Can't we just buy something at a convenience store over there? Or, like, eat at a beachside restaurant?"

"We're leaving early! You're gonna get hungry before we even arrive!"

Me?

"Don't worry—I made something we can eat on the train."

That's not what I'm worried about, though.

"And I ended up making a whole lot, since I thought I should bring enough for everyone."

There were seven people in total: us two siblings, my two childhood friends, Torigoe, Shinohara, and Deguchi.

We didn't need any extras besides Shinohara and Deguchi.

Yeah, I could see why she was up so late if she was making food for that many people.

There weren't many shots to be filmed at the beach, so we could finish by noon if we started early enough.

"You're gonna be doing that till morning if I leave you like this, so here, let me tuck you in."

"No thanks. I'm going to sleep now. Go."

I'm not letting my little sister do that. I'm the older one!

She refused to leave until I was in bed, so I saved whatever progress I had made, shut down the computer, and got in bed.

Still drowsy, I grumbled, "Mana... How did your slap leave a mark on my cheek like they do in manga...?"

"I told you to wake up on time."

I was beyond embarrassed—I felt like a pervert who had just gotten retribution for his debauchery.

Mana had woken me up with a slap, just as promised.

I would have been grateful for my attentive sister for making sure I followed through with my obligations...if only there wasn't that mark on my face.

"People weren't made to wake up at five in the morning..."

My brain was still 70 percent asleep. I had to hurriedly change and brush my teeth, and it wasn't until then that I noticed the mark on my face.

Will it stay like this all day? This is public humiliation.

I kept grumbling under my breath until Mana felt bad and said, "I'll cover it up with foundation." And soon the mark was gone.

She really was a pro at her job. The plain-as-day mark was now practically invisible to anyone who didn't already know about it.

Meanwhile, Fushimi and Himeji arrived. We finished gathering our stuff and left for the train station.

The beach was far, and we needed to transfer trains a few times on the way.

I noticed Fushimi's and Himeji's luggage was bizarrely large as we headed to the station.

"How much are you bringing with you?"

Fushimi opened her raffia bag and showed me its contents.

"A beach blanket, obviously; a beach ball, of course; goggles, a lifesaver…"

You going on vacation, Fushimi?

Her clothes were surprisingly normal this time. A T-shirt, shorts, and sandals. Very ordinary. Had she finally grown up…?

Mana noticed my expression and whispered to me, "I chose that outfit beforehand. I didn't want to be shocked to death first thing in the morning."

A very wise decision.

"Hina…you brought all that?" Himeji said with a sigh, expressing my exasperation as well. "Aren't you forgetting something?"

"What?" Fushimi tilted her head.

"A pump to blow them up."

"Ah! I forgot!"

You could still do it yourself…though it'll be pretty tough.

Fushimi was tearing her hair out when Himeji stretched out her hand.

"Don't worry—I brought one."

You going on vacation, too?!

Mana brought only the food, makeup tools, and a few outfits we might need. I was just carrying the filming equipment.

"…Hina, you're not wearing it under your outfit this time, are you?"

"Huh? Of course I am!"

Fushimi flipped over her T-shirt, exposing what I supposed was her swimsuit.

"Gosh. How come the renowned Hina, prettiest girl in the three kingdoms, acts with such inelegance…?"

Which three kingdoms?

"It's cute. She's like a grade-schooler." Himeji gave her a backhanded compliment.

"Wh-who cares? Dressing rooms are full of strangers; I don't like them."

"Sure, with a body like yours, I would also feel embarrassed if I were to be stared at."

"Ai, shut up or I'm going to flip your skirt in front of Ryou."

"God, she's an actual grade-schooler now."

Stop arguing so early in the morning.

"Relax, Himeji. Don't provoke her," I said to the instigator.

We arrived and got on the train, on our way to the station where we'd meet the other three.

"I thought for sure I would die from waking up so early," said the man with a straw hat and sunglasses.

In his hand, he held the rice ball Mana had made. He soon unwrapped it and started eating.

"Same."

Fushimi, Himeji, Mana, and I met up with Torigoe, Shinohara, and Deguchi on the way, and we were now sitting in the booth seats of the empty train.

"Deguchi, what's with that outfit?"

He was wearing plain shorts and beach sandals. There was nothing odd about his choice of clothing for his lower half.

"What do you mean? You gotta wear this to the beach."

The more you know.

He looked unbelievably smug with the sunglasses. Like he was trying too hard.

Fashion Police Officer Mana ignored it, though. Maybe she just wasn't interested.

I couldn't have him appear as a background character like this, though. I made a mental note to tell Mana to change up his outfit later on. We did bring one change of clothes just in case.

"Your cooking is as good as always, Mana-banana."

That I could agree with. She had brought a few different types of rice balls, along with some side dishes.

Everyone had grabbed their share—the food containers were already empty.

"Good job as always, ManaMana," Torigoe said.

Torigoe and Shinohara were sitting with us. Himeji, Fushimi, and Mana were sitting in the other booth.

""ManaMana?"" Deguchi and I asked in unison.

"She told me to call her that."

Mana called her Shizu, so I guessed that helped her accept using the nickname. Mana probably didn't care about calling anyone anything she wanted.

"Oof... I'm getting nervous now," Shinohara said with a sigh, her face pale. "I can't believe I'll be acting alongside Lady Hime."

"You're the only one who thinks it's such a big deal—relax."

"No, you're the weird one for thinking it's not a big deal." She narrowed her eyes and glared at me.

Hey, don't take out your stress on me now.

"You'll just be having a small conversation; there's no need to get so worked up over it."

She was going to talk to her idol, Aika, and have it filmed. When we'd asked her to be in the scene, she said she was so happy, she might die.

"Curse you... As if being childhood friends with Fushimi wasn't enough, you also get Lady Hime...," she said in a frustrated tone usually reserved for anime characters biting a handkerchief. "I don't care what happens to me; I just want Lady Hime to be happy..."

The difference between how we both treated Himeji was tremendous. I didn't know what to do. She argued against anything I said. What a tiresome fan.

Meanwhile, at the next booth over, Fushimi was merrily looking out the window, Himeji was chiding her, and Mana pointed something out, to which the other two would respond. The cycle repeated again and again.

At least they didn't argue as aggressively when Mana was with them.

"It's the sea! The beach! The sun, the water, and the sand! Bubby, look!"

"I can see; I have eyes."

Mana ran down the stairs onto the sandy beach.

"It's the ocean!!!" Fushimi followed behind her.

After arriving at the station, we had to walk for a bit, and finally, we reached the beach.

I had left it all up to Fushimi and Torigoe, and thanks to that, we ended up in a really remote place.

There was a roadside restroom with two old vending machines beside it.

But there was no convenience store, and the seaside restaurant was closed and covered with a blue tarp.

No dressing rooms, either...but I guess we could just change out of each other's sight?

It was still early morning, and there were barely any people around.

An empty beach was better for filming than a crowded one, for sure, but why had they chosen this place?

I noticed Fushimi was already setting up camp. She laid down the beach blanket and placed her sandals and bag on the corners so it wouldn't fly away.

"Ai, bring me the pump, quick!"

"I'm coming!"

They couldn't wait to start playing around, huh.

"Isn't this heaven? Beautiful girls at the beach under the bright sun…" Deguchi was fanning himself. *Where were you hiding that fan?* "Takayan, soon you'll realize."

"Realize what?"

"Why I am using these sunglasses."

"Right, before anything, we need you to change out of your clothes. You're putting on my most normal, boring clothes."

"What? You serious? This was my outfit for the camera!"

So that's why it looks like that.

"We can't have you in frame dressed like that. It's distracting."

Deguchi chuckled bizarrely. "You hear that, Minami? 'In frame,' he says."

"Wow, you're using cinematography terminology now."

"I am currently a cinematographer, technically."

I had done my research.

Torigoe took off her sandals and stood on the sand.

"Oh, this feels nice…"

I tried doing the same, and it was, in fact, nice. The grains under my soles had a nice texture to them.

Meanwhile, Fushimi and Himeji were already blowing up the beach ball and inner tube.

"Miss Leading Actress! We gotta film! We'll play later!" I shouted.

This apparently flipped a switch within Fushimi.

"Right… I am the leading actress…"

Her expression seemed kinda sad, but Himeji, on the other hand, had on a smug look.

"Go film your scenes already. I'll be preparing things in the meantime."

"Oh yeah, thanks, Ai!"

But our hairdresser and stylist, needed for our leading role's makeup, was already by the shore, merrily exclaiming, "Eep! I got wet! Hee-hee-hee!"

It's over. No one's prioritizing the filming…

"We gotta do what we came here to do first. If we let ourselves play now, we'll just be in trouble later."

I clapped my hands to get everyone's attention, particularly Mana's. We really needed her to do Fushimi's makeup or we couldn't start filming.

"Coming!" Mana answered without much emotion before coming back to the beach blanket.

"Now you're really acting like a director," Torigoe said quietly from beside me as she stared at the ocean.

"I mean, things won't go anywhere if I don't chew them out like this."

"I wasn't being sarcastic like Deguchi and Mii. Really, good job."

"…Oh, thanks."

"I thought you'd be more laid-back."

Fushimi and Mana looked for somewhere to get ready, then hopped onto the seaside restaurant's veranda, disappearing behind the blue sheet.

"I guess that works as a dressing room."

"Huh?" Torigoe wasn't looking, so I pointed at the restaurant, then got back on topic.

"I also thought I'd be more laid-back, but I guess I got influenced by the people who were actually putting in the effort from the beginning."

"You mean Hiina?"

"You too, Torigoe."

She had worked hard to finish the script, and I was involved with it throughout the whole process, so I saw her efforts firsthand.

"So I influenced you."

"You could say that."

She walked through the sand, sandals in hand, and held her hair down from fluttering as she turned her head around.

"Hey, continue filming even after we're done with the shots here."

"What would I film?"

"Us having fun. I don't think we'll be able to gather everyone at the beach again."

I didn't suggest that we could all meet up again another time.

Even if it's what I would've liked, I felt as if, the second I put that into words, this moment would stop being special. And it sounded like Torigoe felt the same.

Had she made that suggestion herself, she knew I would probably say yes.

Despite her actual words being negative, I thought it was a very Torigoe thing to say.

"Put the camera on a tripod so we can film you, too."

"Me too?"

"You are part of my second-year summer. You have to show up."

I walked toward the beach blanket and stood beside her.

"You're being quite enthusiastic, Silent Beauty."

"...Are you making fun of me?"

"I'm not."

"You are."

I put both hands up in surrender, and she kicked the sand at me.

The beach was so empty, I had to wonder if the locals went to some public pool instead.

Maybe it was because of the time of day, but it was too deserted even then.

I mean, even the restaurant wasn't open despite it being peak season.

I stared at Hirono Shibahara through the camera.

Fushimi's head was finally in the game. Not once had her acting failed to meet my expectations.

"Good one," I said as I stopped recording.

"He gave the okay, Fushimi!" Deguchi said through the megaphone.

Her expression changed, and she went back to being the usual Fushimi.

"Can I check it?"

"No, I already okayed it."

"I want to see what you okayed!"

Her enthusiasm ever since we began production was something to greatly appreciate, but honestly, it felt like no one else could keep up with her.

"Being a perfectionist is fine and all, but aren't you just doing it for your self-satisfaction?"

It was the third time I had approved the shot.

"Argh! No!"

No matter how much I, Himeji, or Torigoe said it was fine, this childhood friend kept on rejecting her own shots.

Deguchi, Torigoe, Fushimi, and I looked at the first one I'd okayed. We watched the ten-second shot three times.

"Deguchi, can you tell the difference?"

He glanced at Fushimi and had on the look of an expert.

"Well, when you're on my level, you tend to notice all the little details."

You're just trying to please Fushimi, for Pete's sake.

"See?!" Fushimi said smugly.

Can't you tell he's just saying that...?

"Takamori's already okayed the shot three times," Torigoe said. "Is there something you can clearly tell us you want changed?"

"Yes. The movement of my eyes and the angle of my mouth."

"You wouldn't be able to tell that much on the big screen."

Fushimi couldn't argue back. Torigoe truly never minced her words.

"What you want makes no objective difference from what Takamori already approved."

"It does make a difference!"

"Subjectively, perhaps." I could hear something breaking. "Takamori's the one who understands the full picture. Hiina, ever since we began filming, you've been trying to control everything like it's a one-man show."

"I'm not!"

"There are other things that are more important, so you should try and focus on those instead."

Fushimi shut her mouth tight, its corners progressively curving downward.

"Ai's ready!" Mana exclaimed cheerily as Himeji came out from behind the blue tarp, all dressed up.

…Good timing. Let's change the subject.

"Let's talk about this shot later. Fushimi, take a break. We can still retake it later; the location's not going anywhere."

I noticed Fushimi's eyes and eyebrows tense up. She nodded silently, then turned around and walked toward the beach blanket.

Torigoe let out a tiny sigh. Deguchi glanced back and forth between the two girls.

"W-was that my fault…? Did I mess up by siding with her…?"

"Yes, you technically were the trigger this time, but that problem has been simmering for forever, so don't mind it."

I tried to end the conversation there, but Torigoe was surprisingly worked up.

"As much as you might not believe it, Hiina's an egocentric princess. Indulge her once, and she'll never let up."

Torigoe's words were clearly aimed at me now.

"I'm not indulging her."

"…Sorry. I'm just getting defensive."

The question now was, where did Shinohara go? She said she was just going to go buy a drink.

"Mii's calling for me. I'll be back," Torigoe said after looking at her phone, and she left.

Himeji didn't have many solo scenes, so we were able to finish shooting within twenty minutes.

While checking the footage, Himeji took a sip of one of the drinks Shinohara had bought and carried back with Torigoe, then asked me, "The mood seemed tense; did something happen with Hina?"

"They argued a bit."

"Amateurs," she said. She didn't forget to act all haughty even when trying to be considerate. "We're working as a team. It's not a one-man show where someone can act selfishly."

Her statement rang true, as she used to be part of an idol group.

"How was my acting? We're already on the sixth day of filming, so…"

"There's still a gap between you and Fushimi, but I think it's good."

"I see; I see." She nodded in satisfaction.

I wondered if she was taking that audition for the musical because the project had made her become interested in acting.

"Next we're doing the scene with Eri Akiyama and the background girl."

Shinohara's soft expression stiffened all of a sudden.

"Shinohara, seriously, you'll be fine. Don't think too much about it. You're just a background character. I mean, it's way less embarrassing than your edgy acting back in middle school, right?"

"Stop!" She scowled and walked briskly up to my face. "Don't mention that in front of Lady Hime or I'll bury you right here and now."

Gulp…

Meanwhile, Fushimi was having fun destroying her own sandcastle with a stick.

I'd played that game sometimes in the past. Everyone takes turns sticking a twig inside, and the one who ends up destroying the castle loses.

Was it fun playing that by yourself, though? The point was to compete with multiple people.

Shinohara seemed to have relaxed after our small squabble, so we moved on to shooting the scene.

We did a short rehearsal before filming, to check the angles and how things looked through the finder, and afterward began shooting.

There was this awkwardness to her acting, but it was acceptable.

"You did well, Mii."

"Yeah, you did." I agreed with Torigoe, giving the okay.

As expected from the way she acted in middle school, she had no problem embodying a character.

I did not say that out loud, though. I didn't want to be buried alive.

"Minami, the director's saying you're doing excellent." Deguchi exaggerated my statement through the megaphone.

Himeji nodded.

"Maybe it rings hollow considering my own abilities, but yes, you did great, Minami."

"L-Lady Hime said I'm great…! Th-thank you so, so much…!"

Stop that already. See, now she looks disgusted.

Next, we had to film another solo scene with Fushimi, then the one with Himeji and her.

Hopefully she's ready to move on after the break we gave her…

I turned toward the beach blanket, and there she was, merrily destroying her sandcastle alongside Mana, who had nothing to do now.

I sighed in relief.

When we resumed filming Fushimi's scenes, I decided to be straight and clear with her.

The next shot was when Hirono Shibahara's and Eri Akiyama's suspicions that they are in love with the same person begin taking root.

Torigoe's words must've resonated with Fushimi, as she stopped asking to check the scenes.

"So the first one to realize was Hirono?" Fushimi asked from beyond the camera.

It wasn't written down which one noticed it first, since having it go either way wouldn't have been a problem.

"What do you think?" I asked Torigoe.

She hummed for a bit before saying, "What do you think, Hiina?"

"I feel like it should be Eri instead; it fits her character more."

"Himeji, can you act with that in mind?"

She stood up from the folding chair and brushed away her hair.

"Who do you think I am? Of course I can."

It was amazing she had this much confidence, considering how bad her acting had been before.

Once we had the details in order, Deguchi took away Himeji's chair.

Both Fushimi and Himeji looked serious.

Let's do a rehearsal first.

Then I heard Shinohara from behind say, "You're just making it up as you go, huh."

"Hey, none of us has ever made a movie, so it's only natural."

"Oh, sorry. I didn't mean to criticize you. I meant it in a good way."

"How?"

"You just look like you're having so much fun. My class isn't getting together to make something big like you guys are."

Is that how it looks?

Torigoe and Fushimi kept butting heads, Himeji kept trying to get the upper hand, and Fushimi kept retaliating by giving acting advice to her… My shots were also still shaky despite using a camera with image stabilization.

We were somehow making progress, but I couldn't exactly say things were going swimmingly.

"I should've gone to your high school."

"Nah, smarty-pants should go to schools for smarty-pants."

"Well, sorry for being a genius."

Okay, take it down a notch.

"Hey, seeing as there's nothing around here, what're we gonna eat?" Deguchi asked.

Mana hadn't prepared lunch; we thought we'd be eating at the seaside restaurant. But it was closed.

Having chosen the location, Torigoe said regretfully: "I didn't imagine they'd be closed…"

We hadn't seen any restaurants on our way from the station, either.

"Mind if I go looking for something?" Deguchi asked.

"Okay, then have Mana and Shinohara go with you, since you guys don't have any work to do yet."

"Okay!" Mana said. "Yeah, Degu, the Boss, and I have nothing to do right now."

"Mana, please stop calling me 'the Boss'…"

"Wait, Minami, why's she calling you that?"

"You see," Mana replied.

"You don't need to explain it," Shinohara said.

The three of them chatted as they left the beach.

"Torigoe, why did you choose this place? I mean, it's perfect for filming, but I was wondering."

"…Because…I was worried…"

"About what?"

"About meeting someone I know…if we went to one close by."

"Oh yeah, that probably would've happened had we gone to the nearest beach."

"Just thinking about them laughing and saying, *look at her, she's all energetic in private, ha-ha-ha, nothing like her personality at school,* makes me go red in the face… Or imagine someone from middle school sees me and goes, *wow, she's trying hard to change in high school, so lame.*"

Torigoe…did you…change that much from middle school? You mean you…you're actually cheerier now…?

In the first place, you're acting just like how you normally do at school. You didn't have to worry about that.

"A-anyway, I just didn't want people rolling on the floor laughing at me, which is why I picked this place."

How'd you know they'd be laughing their asses off? You have a serious persecution complex.

But in any case, she seemed to regret her choice due to our current situation.

"Ryou, we're ready!" Fushimi yelled louder than the waves, holding her hands up to her mouth.

"Okay, let's begin."

We had to do some retakes, but filming went relatively well.

I think we went through it faster this time around because Fushimi wasn't asking to check all the shots. It didn't seem like it was because she trusted my judgment now—rather, she was just resisting the urge to check.

We found a supermarket! Mana had sent that text ten minutes ago. They must've found it on the map app and walked all the way there.

It was a good idea sending Deguchi with them, considering they'd have to carry back food and drinks for seven people.

"Shizuka, about the next scene…"

"Yeah?"

With the screenplay in hand, Himeji asked Torigoe something as they sat on the beach blanket.

She was really into it when I remembered she had an audition. There was this greedy feel about the serious look of her side profile.

"I also..."

"What is it, Ryou?"

"Something you wanna ask, Takamori?"

"Nothing." I shook my head.

I was just being influenced by everyone.

It felt like I lacked a sense of self. I don't know how to explain it, but I felt disappointed with myself.

I put the equipment away, making sure sand didn't get inside.

Right, where's Fushimi?

I figured she would've showed up as soon as she heard Himeji asking about the script.

I decided to go for a walk and look for Fushimi while we waited for Mana and the others to return.

"Deguchi was right to wear those flip-flops..."

I'd brought sandals, too, but they weren't made for walking on top of sand.

The only people I could see on this not-so-vast beach were Torigoe and Himeji, who were still talking with each other.

"Is it really the middle of summer here?"

I made a mental note to ask the other person who had chosen this place.

I walked all the way to the other side of the beach, where the rocky area began. Barnacles clung to the rocks, and seaweed swayed about with the waves.

"Heeey! Fushimiii?"

Where is she? I looked around as I stepped on a rock and went farther. I walked alongside the curved barricade and saw a corner full of tetrapods.

"Huh? Have I been here before?"

The scenery gave me a sense of déjà-vu.

We were exploring, then found the tetrapods, and...

I walked toward them while following my memories.

I climbed on the tetrapods and felt the wind. The strong smell of the ocean. I felt the salty breeze stick to my skin.

Among the crashing waves, I heard a familiar voice.

"STUPID RYOU!"

I looked in the direction of the voice, to the side opposite where I came from.

"SIDE WITH ME FOR ONCE!"

Fushimi was breathing heavily.

"What're you doing here?" I called out to her from behind.

"Whoa?!" She flinched and froze in place. "R-Ryou… How long have you been here?"

"I just got here."

I carefully climbed down to her side.

I wanted to ask about what she'd just yelled, but first I had to confirm something.

"We've…been here, right?"

Fushimi blinked in surprise.

"You remember?"

"So we have. I think it was around here where you slipped and fell into the sea."

"…Why do you only remember stuff like that?!" She pouted.

"The water barely reached your waist, but you kept shouting, *'I'm drowning!!'*"

"I—I was just scared, okay?!"

I sat down on the tetrapod and felt the heat it absorbed from the sun pierce my shorts. That and the rough texture made for a terrible chair.

"When was that, first, second grade?"

"Yes, yes we were, Ryou!"

She acted as though an amnesiac friend had suddenly recovered all their memories. She really was that happy.

"Himeji wasn't there, was she?"

"Nope. Ai caught a cold then. We came all the way here for a local children's party when we were in second grade."

There were local events for children like that multiple times a year. They had us visit the sea, hold Christmas parties, and go flower viewing... I wasn't sure if those sorts of things still happened after we grew up, but I went to a lot of them with Mana, Fushimi, and Himeji.

Fushimi crouched down to avoid sitting and dirtying her clothes.

"Was that why you chose this beach?"

Fushimi nodded; she replied while keeping her gaze on the ocean, "I was hoping you'd remember." She giggled. "I'm glad you did.

"So you came here looking for me, huh?" she asked.

"Yeah, I guess."

"Why?"

"Uh…"

Because you disappeared—why else?

I didn't know what to tell her, and after a short silence, she shyly asked me:

"…Were you looking for me to do something dirty?"

"Wha—?!" *How'd you get that idea in your head?!* "Of course not!"

"But y-y-you know, that's a pretty normal situation!"

"Normal where?" *Who gave you that idea?*

"You see it all the time in the movies!"

"What sort of movies are you watching, young lady?"

"You know, the classic scene where a group of friends goes somewhere together, but then the guy and the girl end up all alone, and they start kissing, French kissing, groping each other, and…"

"Okay, stop right there."

That's definitely an R-rated movie. Actually, it sounds like an excuse for a "movie," if you know what I mean… Should you even be watching those?

"And then they find their dead bodies the next day."

"All right, that wasn't what I was picturing."

So a splatter. Okay, I guess that scene is actually pretty cliché, then?

"B-but I'm not saying I wanted you to do that, okay?!"

What if she's just being the classic tsundere…?

No. Don't think about it. She actually looks like she's being honest, waving her hands desperately to avoid misunderstandings.

"But what counts as dirty?"

"Don't ask me."

"Is a kiss considered dirty?"

Didn't you just hear me?

"That's in the gray zone, I think…"

Out of nowhere, Fushimi placed her hand on my cheek and turned my head, making me look straight into her eyes.

"Is gazing into each other's eyes dirty?"

"I don't think so…"

Our shoulders were nearly touching. I never really looked directly at her face, much less at this overwhelmingly close distance, so there was something novel about it despite having known her for so long.

"I don't think a kiss is dirty, either."

She went from an upward glance to holding her chin high. She licked her lips and softly tilted her head.

Then my phone vibrated in objection.

I put my hand into my pocket to check it, but then she grabbed my hand and leaned on me.

"Don't think about anything else but me right now…" Her voice was faint, like a sigh.

Our eyes met, and she looked down. I was sitting cross-legged, and she sat down in the empty space between my legs, then buried her face in my chest.

"Rub my back."

Her ears were burning red.

I stroked her back softly as requested.

©Fly

...Her clothing was thin, and I could feel her bra. I tried hard not to think about it.

"Ryou... I took you by surprise during Golden Week, but..."

"But?"

She grabbed my T-shirt's sleeve tight and pleaded, "Would you like to kiss again, properly, now...?"

My heart had been pounding in my ears even before that, but then it erupted. My mouth was weirdly dry, and my nose couldn't smell anything but the scent of her hair.

There was a warm and soft feel on the back of my hand. I glanced at it and noticed Fushimi's hand was on top of mine.

"I feel like my heart is about to burst..." She gently gripped my fingers. "But it'll be our little secret. No one will know..."

I could feel my face burning up, as though my entire body temperature was concentrating in that spot. My brain wouldn't work. The only other place I felt warmth was where Fushimi was touching.

Fushimi looked up at me with droopy eyes and slowly narrowed them, then closed them entirely.

I took a deep breath. I wasn't sure how long it took me to make up my mind—could've been only an instant, but it also felt like an eternity.

"Hey! Bubby?" I heard a voice from afar the second I had prepared myself mentally.

"Ryou, Mana's calling."

It happened with just the slightest movement. Fushimi reacted to Mana's voice, and my lips touched her cheek. Or rather, they bumped into it.

I messed up.

I didn't know what to do after that. I only heard Mana's voice becoming louder and louder.

"You here? Where are you, Bubby?"

Fushimi held a hand up to her cheek and put on the sweetest, most tender smile before jumping at me with a hug.

"Thank you." She pecked my cheek in return.

She held me tighter before distancing herself.

"Mana's looking for you. Let's go."

She walked back toward the beach, and I followed behind.

Mana was cautiously making her way over the rocks when she found us.

"What were you two doing?"

"Ryou was chewing me out about the filming."

"Really?" She tilted her head and glanced at me.

"Yeah, basically."

"You were totally doing something dirty!"

"We were not," I said.

Though…we did something in the gray zone. I'm technically not lying, though, even if I am bending the truth a bit.

We changed the subject to Mana grumbling about their trip to the supermarket.

"That was way too much walking!"

They had bought a camp stove from a home center, along with cooking utensils, paper plates, chopsticks from a hundred-yen store. And, obviously, food.

"So we're cooking here?"

"Yup. The Boss and Degu are preparing the food as per my instructions right now."

Who's really the boss now?

"Wow, that's our head cook Mana," Fushimi said.

"Hee-hee… I like the sound of that."

What were they going to cook, though…?

"We're making *yakisoba*! Classic beach dish, right?"

"Oh! Yeah, that sounds great!" Fushimi exclaimed.

"Look forward to it!"

The head cook jumped off the last rock and ran merrily toward Shinohara and Deguchi.

I volunteered to help out, but she rejected my offer, saying I'd only cause problems.

Beside the beachside restaurant were three faucets, like the ones you'd see at school. They were cooking right around there.

Fifteen minutes later, the *yakisoba* was done.

"That's the quality of Mana's cooking we've come to expect!"

"Please, praise me more," she beckoned.

We all ate together, and it really was as tasty as always. Despite it just being regular *yakisoba* with nothing special added. Was it because we were eating outside?

"Do you know why it's so good, Takayan?" Deguchi asked, as he gulped down his serving.

"Because Mana made it?"

"That too, but there's more."

"Because of the location?"

"Yup, that's also part of it."

"What else is there?" I was getting impatient.

"Because, besides you and me, we're surrounded by beautiful girls…"

"Wasn't this expensive?" Torigoe asked Mana and Shinohara.

No one was listening to Deguchi. I also pretended as if I didn't hear him.

"It was about seven thousand yen in total. Considering how much a restaurant meal would've cost, I think it's reasonable," Shinohara answered.

So about a thousand yen per person. Yeah, that much would cover a meal and maybe a snack.

"Bubby's gonna pay for my part."

"Who said that?"

"You're the one with a job—don't be stingy!"

"…Fine. Just this once, got it?"

"Hee-hee. I love you, Bubby!"

"Yeah, yeah."

Meanwhile, Fushimi had on this curious expression.

"Ryou, you got a job?"

"Right, I haven't told you. I've been helping an acquaintance of Himeji's."

"Oh." Fushimi glanced at her, then closed her eyes in disinterest.

They handed me the receipt, and I noticed something at the end of the list: FIREWORKS FAMILY SET x 3.

Th-they bought fireworks?!

"Mana, why'd you buy three sets of fireworks?"

"Oh, was that not enough?"

"I'm not asking about the amount. What do we need fireworks for?"

Much to my surprise, no one agreed with me. *Guys, you do realize you could've just paid seven hundred yen each if it wasn't for this? Fourteen hundred in my case.*

"What? I thought my judgment was perfect. I'm pretty sure I made a godly decision by buying them. No, it was even bigger—a cosmic decision."

Cosmic is bigger than godly? Didn't God create the cosmos? Shouldn't it be the other way around?

Nothing good ever came out of commenting on Mana's bizarre wording, though, so I kept my mouth shut.

"We're not even gonna stay here late enough to use them."

""""Huh?"""""

Voices overlapped. I soon learned everyone responded in the same manner, as I noticed all of them giving me weird looks.

It was barely past one in the afternoon; I couldn't imagine us staying here for that much longer.

All the girls, though, immediately put the food utensils away. They changed and equipped swimming rings, dove into the ocean, and started playing and giggling.

I kept myself amused by grabbing sand. Deguchi stayed beside me, wearing his sunglasses and staring into the distance.

"Deguchi, is looking at the horizon that fun?"

"That's what you would think, wouldn't you, Takayan? Oh, but you are wrong."

"What do you mean?"

"The sunglasses hide my gaze. Which gives me the opportunity to freely ogle their swimsuits. They wouldn't know I'm staring at them."

"That's why you brought them…?"

Couldn't you use that passion for something more productive? I sighed, but at the same time, I was slightly impressed by how far he'd thought ahead.

"My man…this is the main dish of the day. See, I'm the one who should be sighing. How could you even for a second consider leaving as soon as we were done filming? Who knows when we'll get an opportunity like this again!"

"I guess."

We did have to start focusing on studying for our college entrance exams next year, so we likely wouldn't have the time to play around like this.

"Join us, Ryou!" Fushimi beckoned me.

She was wearing a one-piece swimsuit with a floral design. It looked like a minidress, and I would've asked her, *Aren't you worried your underwear might show?* if I didn't know it was a swimsuit.

"Torigoe, what about you?" I asked the girl behind me who was reading a book.

She was sitting just under the restaurant's shade. She had changed but was wearing a thin hoodie, with the hood on.

"I got to a really good part in this novel just before we arrived, and it's been gnawing at me this whole time. So I'm good for now," she said.

"Her outfit's crazy, don't you think?" Deguchi whispered while still facing forward.

"How?"

"I know she's got a swimsuit underneath, but otherwise, she's wearing nothing under that hoodie, right?"

"I suppose?"

"And because of that hoodie, it makes you feel like her swimsuit's actually just her underwear...and she's flashing them like it's nothing."

"Oh, for... Don't put it like that, idiot! Now you're making me see it that way."

"HA-HA-HA!" Deguchi cackled while fanning himself. "I knew you would get it, Sir Takayan."

"Please don't."

The colorful beach ball splashed into the sea, and there was giggling all around.

Himeji was wearing the swimsuit she had bought that day, while Shinohara was wearing her school's bathing suit. Maybe because it was from a private school, it looked like professional swimwear. She was still wearing her glasses and had her hair tied up.

"Bubby, come over here!" Mana called out to me after realizing I wasn't responding to Fushimi's invitation. "Everyone knows you're terrible at this game—don't worry about it!"

"I'm not worried about that!"

Deguchi heaved a heavy sigh. "The problem's Mana-banana."

"What? Why?"

"She's in middle school, right? Yet look at that body. That's not fair. That's cheating. A *gyaru* who's a good cook, is obsessed with her brother, and has those melons? Geez."

It did not sit right with me having him talk about my sister that way.

"Oh, excuse me. Those aren't melons. It's summer, after all—they're watermelons."

"Who cares, dude?"

The most shocking comment, actually, was that apparently to others, it looked as if Mana had a brother complex?

"Ryou! Come over here already!"

Deguchi talked passionately about Himeji's body as well. I let most of it go in one ear and out the other, but I did hear the word *grapes*. *What's with you and fruits, man?*

It didn't seem like we were going home anytime soon, so I sluggishly got up. Better than just staring, I supposed.

I had brought a swimsuit, since Mana wouldn't shut up about it, so I changed behind the blue tarp.

"I'm gonna join them, Deguchi."

"Takayan, may I ask one last question before you go?"

"Yeah?"

"Why did no one call for me to join them…?"

I couldn't tell because of his sunglasses, but I imagined he was really staring into the horizon this time.

"Because you do crap like hide your gaze behind sunglasses."

Deguchi fell down on the sand in pain.

The beach ball came rolling my way. I picked it up and tossed it back into the sea as I joined the girls.

By the time I realized it, the beach was tinted in orange, and the sky was growing darker.

I recorded us playing around, just as Torigoe had suggested.

And we played for several hours. Beach volleyball turned out to be more fun than I'd expected.

I wondered how long it had been since the last time I used my voice until it was hoarse.

When I thought about how my frolicking had been caught on camera, it made me want to never look at the footage.

Partway through, Torigoe joined us for beach volleyball, and we played in teams of two of various pairings.

When Shinohara and I were paired together, the Torigoe and Fushimi team turned strangely aggressive.

As for Deguchi, no one invited him for hours on end. Poor guy got lonely. I suggested we all play beach flags, but none of the girls agreed. I think they realized Deguchi only wanted to stay back and observe from the opposite side of the runners. So, in the end, the guy ended up playing by himself.

I couldn't bear the sight of that and, since I was getting hungry anyway, I suggested we go buy something. I figured, even for drinks, it'd be more cost-efficient to grab a big bottle at the supermarket than buy the individual ones from the vending machines.

"What are you, Takayan? A housewife?"

"Tell that to Mana and she'd be like, *Uh, duh?* while giving you the scariest glare ever. Choose your words carefully."

"Oh, that sounds nice."

Yeah, I forgot this guy was fine with anything.

I took out my wallet at the register, since it was me who had suggested coming here, but then Deguchi offered to split the bill.

By the time we got back to the beach, it was dark, and the girls were already preparing the fireworks.

"Oh man, they changed…" Deguchi sighed.

I could barely see at all, but it seemed he had a sensor for this sort of thing—he could immediately tell they were back to wearing regular clothes.

See, Deguchi, that's why no one invites you to join them.

It was too windy for candles, so we lit them up with the stove.

Fushimi and Mana were extremely excited about it, despite just having played with fireworks during Golden Week. Torigoe seemed excited, too—she cheerily stared into the lights of the fireworks.

This reminds me of that kiss...

Fushimi had said that was unfair to her. That she wasn't as nice a girl as I thought.

I had no idea what she meant, but Himeji had said something similar. Apparently, there was a concept of fairness when it came to these things.

If that was true, then perhaps it really was Fushimi who wrote that stuff in my notebook about having my first kiss with her once I got into high school.

It was written after Himeji transferred schools. Around when we were still writing letters to each other.

I had a recollection of the letters, and I was sure I had them stored somewhere. But our feelings must have been mutual since I continued to correspond with Himeji.

We used up nearly all the fireworks while I was lost in thought. Only sparklers remained.

"Three was the perfect amount," Torigoe told Mana.

"Right? I knew one wouldn't be enough! I'm glad I convinced you!"

Deguchi was recording everything with the camera. I'd told him to be extremely careful with it, since it wasn't ours, and he seemed to be doing a fine job.

"The sea at night is…quite something, isn't it?"

"What do you mean?"

My sparkler's spark fell with the wind.

"Oh, nothing." Himeji refused to explain herself. "Deguchi, you should avoid recording the sea itself."

"Huh? Why?" Deguchi was still holding the camera, even though he was already picking up the trash and preparing to leave.

Everyone turned their attention toward Himeji.

"What if it happens to capture...*something?*"

Silence fell. A chilly wind blew.

"Himejima, let's not say that sort of thing, okay?"

The wind blew stronger, ruffling the blue tarp loudly.

"Meowa!" Fushimi screamed like a frightened cat.

Her scream scared me, and Shinohara and Torigoe ran away in silence. It was pandemonium already.

"What?! Wh-what is it?!"

Even Mana, who usually stayed calm no matter what, panicked. This only scared everyone even more. She tugged at my hand, trying to pull me away from the coast.

"Bubby, w-we g-g-gotta go!"

"Wait, hold on! Everyone... Is something here?! T-Takayan, wait for me!" Deguchi ran after us.

Wait, where's Fushimi?

I turned around and saw her frozen in place.

This can't be good!

"Fushimi." I turned back, but Mana tried to stop me. I dragged her with me all the way back to Fushimi, and I grabbed her arm.

"I—I just saw something...," Himeji said as she ran right by us.

"Bubby, we gotta go!"

"Fushimi! Fushimi, c'mon!"

"Ah... Ryou?"

"We're leaving!"

Mana gripped my hand, and I gripped Fushimi's, and we ran for our lives.

...We arrived at the station in no time. I was short of breath, and my sandals had nearly come off multiple times on the way.

The rough feeling of sand remained on my feet.

We were the last ones to get there. Everyone else welcomed us with worried looks.

"…So what did you see?" Deguchi asked to no one in particular.

"I don't know," I said.

"Hee-hee." Mana giggled. "You were all so panicky. It was funny."

"Mana, this is no laughing matter! I was so scared, I couldn't move!"

"Hina, maybe you couldn't move because someone was grabbing your feet…"

"DON'T SAY THAT!"

I couldn't tell if it was a reaction to this sense of relief or because I was no longer scared, but I began to laugh.

"I was so, so scared, seriously…" Fushimi started tearing up.

Torigoe, Shinohara, and I laughed.

"What happened back there, really?" Himeji feigned ignorance.

…It was all because of you. You scared everyone.

"Geez, I was terrified, too," Deguchi said while cackling.

We kept on laughing in the otherwise deserted station for a while, and we missed the train.

"Wait… It's thirty minutes until the next one! What is this, the middle of nowhere?!"

"You just realized?" I replied to Deguchi's annoyed comment, and everyone laughed. Anything could make us chuckle at that point.

We waited until the next train and were finally on our way back home.

We chatted at first, but soon enough, the swaying of the train made everyone fall asleep.

"Ryou, you're not sleepy?"

"I just wanna check the footage."

"Oh." Fushimi giggled.

"By the way, I'm pretty sure Himeji made up that thing about the ghost."

©Fly

"Huh?" Fushimi's eyes turned into dots. She whipped around to face Himeji, who was sound asleep by her side, and pinched her cheeks. "Looks like this dirty, deceitful mouth needs washing!"

No matter how hard she pinched, though, Himeji showed no sign of waking up.

Fushimi leaned back in the seat again and let out a weary sigh of relief before grunting:

"Oh. Mwoh?!"

"What?"

"I auditioned for a play and...look!"

Fushimi shoved her phone in my face with a dazzling expression.

There was an email, and the subject line read, Preliminary Selection Results. She was informed that she had passed the first screening.

"It's only the first step, though—they just reviewed my documents. But still." She could barely contain her smile.

"...You gotta wait for an email for that?"

"Don't question their ways, okay?"

I think I was feeling jealous of her again. Why couldn't I just say congratulations first?

"...Good for you, Fushimi. Congratulations."

"Yes. Thank you, thank you. I want to thank all the people in the world!"

She was more hyper than usual.

Meanwhile...what did I have?

Like Himeji and Fushimi, what could I put my all into?

I didn't want something to brag about, nor did I aim to surpass someone. I just wanted something to share with other people like that...

"While practicing, my teacher told me..." Fushimi explained how she had gotten into the audition. There were four screenings to go through before actually being selected. "I applied online, and I also linked the social media account we made recently. I think that worked in my favor!"

Pretty modern of them to use social media as a reference.

"It's all thanks to you and Shii," she said in all seriousness.

"I don't think we did anything."

"Really?" *Really.* "Look at me."

"Huh? Okay?"

"I want you to cheer me on."

"Of course I will."

"Thank you." She smiled innocently, and I could only look away.

She said she was unfair and a bad girl, but honestly, I was sure I was much worse.

"Just knowing you're rooting for me gives me the strength to do anything!"

Just today, she had climbed up many steps; there was a fire burning within her. All while remaining as diligent as always—she reassured me she would still give her all to the film.

Once back home, I washed away the sweat and salt residue from the ocean in the shower, all while looking back on what had happened during the day. A lot went on as we spent the day filming and playing on the beach, but what remained strongly in my mind was the conversation with Fushimi on the train.

I finished showering and went back to my room.

I tried thinking about something else, in an attempt to forget the shapeless, heavy weight on my chest.

I tried reading the manga I'd started recently, then a movie I was recommended; then I just tried thinking about anything else, but no matter what, the thought came back to me like a boomerang.

I fiddled around with Mr. Matsuda's camera. The battery was running low; I had to charge it.

At first I thought it'd be too much for me to handle, but now I was entirely used to operating it. I mean, I wasn't a perfect cameraman, but I knew how to use the thing.

"I…"

Why don't I have anything?

Just as the thought crossed my mind, I felt as though the camera in my hands was trying to tell me something.

I took out the SD card full of recordings for our film and changed it for a new, blank one.

I grabbed my pencil case and took out a mechanical pencil and started writing down whatever came to mind on my classical literature notebook that was just lying around.

It was past midnight by the time I checked the clock.

Don't think you have nothing.
Think about how you could achieve something.

My classical literature notebook was mostly empty; I didn't usually take a lot of notes. But now it was full of my thoughts.

I was sure I'd be puzzled at why I even wrote all that once the heat of the moment passed.

Soon it was morning, and I kept holding that pencil until it was noon, and before I realized it, Mana came back with dinner.

I was writing what would surely come to be categorized as a dark past I wouldn't want to look back at, but that was fine. I'd had no dark or light up to then—I had nothing.

I had no plans for the next day, so I just wrote in my notebook the whole time, spitting out everything I had thought of.

"Bubby, you seem a bit on edge… What's going on?" Mana tilted her head, chopsticks in her mouth.

"Nothing."

"Ah! It's your rebellious phase!"

"Shut up!"

Just trying to dodge a question doesn't make me an edgy teenager—come on.

I finished dinner, took a shower, and went back to my room to continue writing in my notebook.

Once it was entirely full (of which only ten pages were about classical literature), I read it over again.

It was full of cringey content, to be quite honest. There was no rhyme or reason to my writing. It was bitter and embarrassing. Undecipherable even to me.

But I felt a consistent passion in those words.

It took no time for me to wish to turn it into a film.

I could understand now why Fushimi kept her goal to become an actress a secret.

"Hard at work, I see, Ryo-Ryo!"

Filming ended before noon, and I had gone to my afternoon part-time job. Mr. Matsuda was just returning to his office, bag in hand.

"Hello, Mr. Matsuda."

He had gone from calling me Ryou to the nickname Rio, and now, somehow, Ryo-Ryo.

"Oof, today was a long day!" He sighed before plopping down in his chair and reclining it all the way back.

He was deliberately doing all that in the hopes that I'd ask what happened.

I thought he should say whatever he wanted to say himself, instead of trying to get me to ask him about it.

I felt he was too good-looking for that sort of personality.

"Sure is, huh," I replied mechanically.

Mr. Matsuda sat up and said, "Gosh, Ryo-Ryo, you're so cold!"

"Did something happen, sir?" I succumbed.

His plans for that morning included a meeting with a video production company for a commercial.

I had been asked to answer calls on top of emails and messages, so I was starting to know his entire schedule.

"Their director just doesn't understand. The man doesn't get it."

"That must have been tough."

"It made me wish it was you directing instead."

"Huh?" That caught me off-guard.

"I'm kidding."

"Y-yeah…"

A staff member brought him barley tea, and he gulped it down in one go.

"Aika told me your film's going great."

"Yes, all thanks to you. I know how to use the camera well now, and it has been of great help."

"Oh, no need to thank me. In fact, I should be thanking you for everything."

That thing about me positively influencing Himeji?

I still couldn't believe that; she was already very positive from the moment we met again.

"How are things going with her audition, by the way?"

"Mm, wanna know?"

"I suppose. She told me about it, but I don't want to ask her directly in case she didn't do well."

"I understand. She's been doing well. I knew that girl had it in her." *Good. Hopefully she does get into that musical.* "She just has to pass the fourth screening and…"

"Wait, fourth?"

I'd heard of a similar system recently.

"Something wrong?"

"That audition's the sort of thing professionals apply to, right?"

"Well, professionals attached to an agency are seeded, if we're to use sports terminology—they start from the second round. But people in general can apply from the first stage, and sometimes they end up going all the way to the final screening. Thing is, though, ninety-nine percent of the people drop out at the documentation stage."

So amateurs are also allowed…and their documents are reviewed…

"Are there other similar auditions going on?"

"What's up today? You're quite interested, huh." Mr. Matsuda opened his eyes wide. "For auditions where they're looking for a woman in her teens with acting and singing chops to play the lead role, then there's only that one this summer."

Then the audition Fushimi was talking about is...

"And she's so fired up right now. I hope she makes it past the last screening. She still isn't entirely up to par in acting, but still."

I wasn't even listening by that point.

I had received a text from Fushimi just ten minutes before Mr. Matsuda came back, saying, I passed the third screening! Let's goooooooo! Time for the last one!!!

I felt someone tap my shoulder. I turned around and saw Deguchi pointing with his chin.

Oh, right.

I hurriedly stopped recording.

"Okay!" I said.

Deguchi clapped in lieu of a clapperboard.

"He says it's good. You can rest now."

"Got it!" Fushimi replied to Deguchi's voice.

We were shooting a scene in the classroom, but I was lost in thought about what I'd found out the other day.

I'd replied back to Fushimi, telling her congratulations and good luck, but...neither of them knew about the other, huh?

"Ai, compared to when we practiced, let's try keeping some more distance between us as we speak, okay?"

"Why? You don't want me near you?"

"Gosh! No, it's for the scene!"

"...Can we practice that first?"

"Hee-hee. I knew you'd do it."

"Enough teasing—let's just start already."

Just as Mr. Matsuda had said, Himeji's acting was still lacking when compared to Fushimi's.

But she knew that. Which was why she accepted Fushimi's advice.

After all, Fushimi was going to acting school. Himeji had said she was also taking voice training lessons at some studio, but it was mainly for the purposes of her audition.

Both of them wanted my support. I couldn't just side with either of them. I wished them both good luck.

But considering it was for the lead role, naturally only one of them could win. Though I'd heard that two people could get the same role depending on the number of shows.

Fushimi had told me the date for her last screening, and it aligned with the day for Himeji's that I'd heard from Mr. Matsuda.

They would likely bump into each other at the venue.

I got anxious all of a sudden…but why?

I guess they could both fail, too. I shouldn't worry too much about it.

That scene we just shot was the last one for today.

The classmates we rounded up as extras all said good-bye, citing their empty stomachs.

Himeji said she had plans (probably the voice training), and Fushimi said she had acting lessons, so only Deguchi, Torigoe, and I remained.

"Wanna go grab a bite somewhere?" Deguchi asked.

We went to the convenience store for some food and brought it to the cafeteria that was still open to eat. I got rice balls.

"How's production going? We nearly done?"

"Filming is nearly done."

"Nice!" Deguchi exclaimed.

Torigoe drank her juice while shaking her head. She took her mouth off the straw and said, "But Takamori still has to edit, add music, and all that."

"…Wha—? So you gotta work more than anyone else, Takayan?" *I suppose.* "Then what's the progress like, in general?"

"I'd say we're, um, halfway through?"

"Oof… Are we…really gonna make it?"

Torigoe answered in my stead, with full confidence, "We will. He will."

At least let me say that.

"Good luck, then, Takayan."

"Thanks," I said flatly.

"Oh, also, what about *that*?"

"Right. *That*." I immediately knew what he was talking about.

"What do you mean?" Torigoe asked, confused.

"Remember how we went to the beach with everyone? Since I got footage of us, I was thinking of making a video with it."

Torigoe's eyes turned cold and lifeless as she heard my answer.

"You're making a video of everyone in swimsuits?"

I knew this would happen. This is why I didn't want to do it.

"No, no, no, Torigoe, this is about preserving our memories. A video album of our youth. We will look back on it years later in nostalgia. We'll look back on the past over some drinks and stuff," Deguchi hurriedly explained.

You and I both know that's not your real aim.

"I was also thinking I wanted a video of it, but just picturing Takamori combing through the clips while editing all alone…" Her voice trailed off.

"I don't think you have to worry that much. You were wearing that hoodie the whole time. And I will hold that against you for the rest of my life."

Who do you think you are, man?

"I can't expose myself in front of Himeji and ManaMana…"

So you don't want to be compared to them, huh. And you just implied you didn't care about being compared to Fushimi, huh.

"Fret not! I can say with full confidence that what you have is perfectly—"

"Shut up, idiot. You walking lump of sexual harassment." I cut him short.

"But look at those legs, dude!"

"Just shut up, please."

I totally agree, though.

Torigoe choked up.

"Uh, so, anyway. I assure you, I'm not going to do anything weird, Torigoe. I'm just gonna put the clips together."

"Okay. Fine, then."

Permission granted.

We couldn't even bring the topic up without Deguchi getting weird about it, geez.

The guy then said he had plans for the evening and left right after finishing his lunch.

Torigoe only bought a juice. I asked if that was enough for her, and she simply answered that she was feeling fatigued from the heat.

I had never experienced heat exhaustion, so I wasn't sure how concerning that was. She explained eating would only make her feel worse, which only made me more confused.

Just as Torigoe was close to finishing her juice, we ran out of topics to discuss. So I asked her something that had been on my mind the whole time.

"Hey, Torigoe, I want you to do me a favor."

"Hmm?"

"Would you star in my film?"

"Wha—?" Torigoe blinked.

I explained further. "Not the movie we're making for school. A personal film of mine."

"…" She stayed frozen in disbelief for a few seconds before saying, "No."

I knew that would happen. She wasn't the kind of person to happily agree to such a request.

"Why ask me? You have Hiina and Himeji."

"You're the best choice for the character."

"Me?"

I nodded.

I had organized all the messy ideas I wrote down in my notebook and mimicked what Torigoe did to make a screenplay of my own. The protagonist turned out to be a perfect fit for Torigoe. Fushimi, Himeji, or Mana wouldn't have worked.

I'd thought about asking Mr. Matsuda if he knew someone, but I felt too shy to ask an actual professional attached to an agency to work with me.

Torigoe didn't say yes even after I explained all this.

"I seriously can't do it. I'm not half as good as Himeji."

"I see…"

I mean, I figured Fushimi could still play the part, since she had the acting skills, but I was sure she couldn't empathize with the actual character.

Torigoe was just perfect for it… But, well, I can't force her…

"Okay, then how about…"

She couldn't bear to see me troubled anymore and suggested:

"…you try to w-woo me?"

"What?"

"T-try to woo me into wanting to do it."

I see—she wants me to show just how passionate I am about the project.

"Also, did you tell Hiina about this?"

"Nope."

"Tell her."

"Why? It's just a personal project of mine."

"If I end up saying yes, I want it to be under fair conditions."

Fair conditions?

I repeated the phrase in my mind. I didn't get it.

"What's it about? I never thought you'd ask me something like this, so I'm curious."

"It's hard to explain, but, um…"

I wasn't sure I explained it well; I feared I wasn't getting my idea across.

Yet Torigoe listened attentively, sometimes asking me questions. It was like we switched places from when she had been creating the film for the school festival.

"That sounds good."

"Y-you think?"

It felt like the soft light of salvation was shining upon my bundle of weaknesses, and embarrassment.

"Yes, I like it."

"W-wow. Thank you."

I sighed in relief, and she smiled.

"So…do your best trying to woo me."

I had no idea how I was supposed to "woo her." I tried looking it up online, but none of the results seemed useful to me. I just had to approach her and figure it out for myself.

However, due to scheduling issues, we had to pause filming for a week.

We had no reasons to meet up; I just called her on the phone sometimes to talk about my film.

I didn't feel as anxious about talking to her after she'd said she liked the story. That was a huge relief.

"You're amazing, Torigoe," I said once there was a pause in our conversation; I felt like my worries were swept away.

"Huh? Why?"

"You're just easy to talk to."

"…Um… Uh… You think?" Her voice lowered. *"I didn't expect you to go for that route in trying to woo me."*

"Huh?"

"Nothing, forget it."

Our calls mostly went like that.

Then I told her Fushimi would be coming over to do homework the next day, and she said, *"I'm good. Thanks for inviting me, though."*

It was the day of the audition.

Fushimi and I were heading to the venue. We had to transfer trains many times on the way.

"You doing well, Fushimi?"

"Yes. I'll be fine."

"Okay."

I was nervous.

I kept my phone in my hand, looking at it, then putting it back in my pocket before taking it out again and checking if I had any notifications.

"…You don't seem to be doing well, though." She giggled.

"I'm just nervous."

"Whoa! For me?"

"I don't get it myself."

"Okay?" She beamed.

She wasn't mentioning Himeji. Nor was the latter mentioning the former.

They really didn't know. They had no idea that the other was taking the final test for the same audition.

Himeji wasn't talking about the audition at all, in fact. I knew she passed the earlier rounds only thanks to Mr. Matsuda. It was no surprise, considering how obstinate and prideful she was. She probably thought she'd end up ridiculed if she failed in the end.

We got off at our destination, and Fushimi led me to the venue while checking her phone for directions.

She was holding a parasol, so it felt cool on our walk there.

"It's only twelve of us for this last audition. Crazy, right?" she said in a casual tone.

It sounded like she didn't expect to have gotten this far.

"I thought I wouldn't be able to sleep last night, but that wasn't the case at all. Ha-ha-ha." She looked strangely cheerful and was more talkative than on our way to and from school. "Sorry for making you come all the way here on such a hot day. My dad was supposed to come, but it turned out he had to work. I guess I could've come by myself, but, well…"

"You'd be too distracted that way?"

"Huh?"

"Oh, nothing." I took out a bottle of water I'd bought at a convenience store on the way. I opened it up and passed it to her. "You thirsty?"

"Oh, thanks." She took two sips, then exhaled deeply.

We walked through an unfamiliar business district, then through a small side street. Who wouldn't feel anxious in such a secluded part of an unknown location?

We stopped before a very normal-looking building. The windows strongly reflected the sun's light.

"The studio's on the third floor." Fushimi stared at the third floor of the building, as did I.

She took a deep breath. She had to be way more nervous than I was.

"Oh, your water." She handed it back, but I shook my head.

"Take it with you. You didn't buy anything for yourself."

"Right. Okay, thank you. It's time, then." She waved before entering the building.

Now I had to kill time around here until they finished. But just as I was thinking that, I heard a familiar voice.

"Ryou...?"

"Hmm? Oh, Himeji."

Of course she'd arrive at around the same time.

Mr. Matsuda was with her, too.

"Why are you here?"

"I, uh, um..." What could I say? She really didn't know about Fushimi.

"You looked up the venue for the audition and came all the way here... Seems like you're a natural stalker, Ryou."

"I'm not!"

Mr. Matsuda cleared his throat. "I asked Ryo-Ryo to come here to surprise you."

No you didn't?!

"Really?!" Himeji turned around to look at him, then immediately turned back to me.

I narrowed my eyes, staring at the liar; he mouthed to just go with it, then winked.

"Uh, yeah, pretty much."

Himeji's stiff expression softened in absolute joy.

But then she immediately shook her head.

"Thank you for coming on such a hot day. I, I did tell you to root for me, but I didn't expect you to come all the way here. I'm so glad...errr... no, I..."

"Break a leg, Himeji."

"I—I don't need your good luck! I'm going to crush that audition!" she said before going in.

Mr. Matsuda sighed in relief once she was out of sight.

"Good job, Ryo-Ryo. Well done."

*   *   *

Mr. Matsuda and I went to a nearby café. We sat across from each other at the table.

We each ordered an iced coffee.

He sighed before saying, "I felt she wasn't doing so well today…but then she got fired up the moment she saw you."

"Oh, so that's why you told me good job."

"Yup."

They had come here together from the office, and she was restless the whole way. Mr. Matsuda was worried sick.

"She was like a bunny shivering before a wolf."

"That's surprising. I thought she'd be used to this sort of thing, considering her experience as an idol."

"I'm sure she wouldn't be worried about an audition in that line of work, but it is her first time for this kind of job, and she's been working hard for it." He stirred the coffee with his straw, the ice clinking against one another. "But then the little bunny turned into a woman the moment she saw you. I was shocked."

"I'm shocked about you lying to her."

"By the way, why are you here, really? I don't imagine you were actually waiting for her."

"Oh… Well, you see…" I finally explained why I had been asking him so much about Himeji's progress.

"Oh, so you came with your childhood friend?"

"Yeah."

"And she's an amateur…? No agency?"

"I don't think so, no."

"Oh my. It's that girl I've been hearing about. Everyone's talking about the newbie."

Mr. Matsuda had told me 99 percent of applicants fail at the first stage. It was beyond rare for someone starting from the bottom to climb all the way to the top.

She's quite something…

"Childhood friends and classmates, huh… I see," Mr. Matsuda muttered while looking in the direction of the venue.

◆Hina Fushimi◆

I took a sip of water from the bottle Ryou had given me.

I was restless.

I tried looking at my phone, but I stopped myself so I wouldn't lose focus. I took my hand off my bag and placed it back on the desk.

I was in the waiting room twenty minutes before the appointed time. There were a couple more people there. One girl seemed to be in middle school, but she was really pretty. The other looked about my age, but she seemed quite mature. They appeared just as restless.

"Good morning." The door opened, and another cute girl entered. "Let's do our best." She bowed.

Our eyes met after she lifted up her head.

It was Ai.

I felt relief at the sight of a familiar face, but just as I was about to call out to her, she recognized my face and put on a serious expression.

She walked right by me and whispered, "I won't lose."

"I won't, either," I replied.

I was vaguely aware she was an idol, but this confirmed it. I'd heard her say things suggesting so when we'd gathered at Ryou's house for the planning meeting.

I felt like it was fate.

Who would've thought we'd both apply to the same audition and reach the final screening?

Maybe one of us would pass. Perhaps we'd both fail.

But we couldn't both win.

I didn't want to compete with her even on this. I felt we were better off both failing. That'd be easier on us.

But I really didn't want to lose.

After claiming her future victory, Ai sat on the chair farthest from me. I was hoping to chat and relax; why'd she have to sit all the way there? I felt like I was about to suffocate from the pressure.

Finally, the time arrived. A young man entered the waiting room.

"Good morning, all."

Everyone greeted him back. I found it curious, ever since Ai herself said it. It was surprising to find out people in the entertainment industry really said "good morning" as their fixed greeting even when it wasn't morning.

I gave my greeting later than everyone else; then he started explaining the process.

We were going to be called according to our entry number and go through the screening in another room. The first girl was called right away, and she left with the man.

She came back fifteen minutes later. Then the second girl was called and also came back fifteen minutes later, then the third girl. I knew my own entry number, obviously, but I didn't know everyone else's. It could be a while.

Then it was Ai's turn. She stood up and left the room. I cheered for her in my mind.

The man returned fifteen minutes later.

"Next up is Hina Fushimi."

"Y-yes!"

"They're still in the middle of it, but it'll end soon. Let's go."

"Yes," I replied again before giving myself a couple of little slaps on the face.

I walked out to the hallway and saw Ai just coming out of the room and bowing.

She reached her hand out to me just as we were about to pass each other. I responded in kind and high-fived her.

"Break a leg."

"Thanks."

The guy looked back in confusion.

"You know her?"

"Yes. We're childhood friends and classmates."

"Wow." He stopped before the door. "Go in when you're ready."

I took a deep breath.

Then I thought back on the career survey paper I'd submitted.

...I will do it. I'll make it.

I'll pass this audition and become an actress.

◆Ryou Takamori◆

Mr. Matsuda got a text from Himeji, and he told her we were in the café. I received a text from Fushimi soon after.

"I want to meet this childhood friend of yours," he said.

So I asked her to come to the café and told her Himeji was coming, too. We were hearing about the audition from Himeji when Fushimi arrived.

"Huh? It's her? That's her?" Mr. Matsuda asked. I nodded. "Oh. My. Gosh. She's so cute! So cute!"

Okay.

Fushimi noticed us and waved, then furrowed her brow as soon as she saw Mr. Matsuda.

"This is Mr. Matsuda, the manager at the office I've been working at."

"He's the chief manager of my agency," Himeji added.

"Oh, is that so? It's a pleasure to meet you. I'm Hina Fushimi." She quickly introduced herself.

"You're amazing, Fushimi! You got all the way to the last screening from the documentation step!"

"Oh, it's nothing… Ah-ha-ha."

Himeji used a straw to take a sip of her juice.

"I had heard you were going to an acting school, but I never expected to meet you at the venue for an audition I was taking."

"Right? I was shocked, too."

"Yeah."

Mr. Matsuda stared at Fushimi every time she spoke. It was as though he was surveying her, like he was trying to absorb every tiny detail about her.

The final screening was nothing like I had imagined. It was mostly small talk and some questions, including their goals for the future. It was the same for Fushimi and Himeji.

"I'll have one of those!" Fushimi said while looking at Himeji's mixed fruit juice.

She came back with her own glass on a tray.

"So you don't act or sing for this review, huh."

"We already did that for the second and third screenings."

Oh. No need to check that again, then.

"They film each round to review how they acted later on," Mr. Matsuda added.

It made sense why the last one was more like an interview.

Fushimi and Himeji stayed quiet once that topic was over. They must've been curious about the results.

"No point in worrying about it now. Just forget you even took the audition in the first place, honestly," Mr. Matsuda said.

Then he asked if we had any plans after this. We said no, and he offered to take us home in his car.

I got in the back seat of the luxury sedan. Fushimi followed behind me, while Himeji got in from the other side.

I whispered for one of them to sit in the front, but it seemed they didn't hear me. They stayed in the back.

Mr. Matsuda glanced at me from the rearview mirror and chuckled.

"Surrounded by beauties, I see. Goddesses, even," he said jokingly.

The girls on either side soon fell asleep. They must've been super tired. A good part of the ride went by in silence.

"Try stealthily recommending my agency to Fushimi, okay, Ryo-Ryo?"

"Stealthily?"

"I mean, like, don't go and tell her, *Hey, wouldn't it be nice if you worked with Aika?* We're not a local sports team."

I chuckled.

It seemed the producer had taken an interest in Fushimi.

Your protagonist energy never fails to surprise me.

She had passed the supposedly impossible documentation stage and reached the final stage. It felt like she could even easily win the lead role.

"…Why do you look so frustrated?"

"Huh? Was I making that sort of face?"

"Yes, you looked green with envy."

"I'm not jealous. I don't want to be a celebrity."

"I mean, not envious of that, but of being recognized in general."

That hit me hard.

"Well, you are at that age. Hey…please show me that film you're making, yes?"

"I don't mind, but it's nowhere near complete yet."

"Look, I'm not an expert in that field, but I do know what the real professionals have in mind when producing movies. I could teach you a thing or two."

"I—I would be extremely grateful. I'll bring what we have next time, then."

"Gooood!" he said in a singsong voice.

August came, and just as we were about to resume filming, Fushimi messaged our production group chat:

Sorry, I'm not feeling well today. Could we postpone the
shoot?

Before I could say anything, many of our classmates replied telling her
to rest and take care.

Filming was soon to wrap up, and Fushimi was passionate about the
project to an annoying degree. Honestly, I couldn't imagine her asking to
take a day off.

Despite my doubts, I sent her a private message telling her to rest up
and that she didn't have to worry about the project.

Sorry and thanks, she replied.

Himeji and Torigoe didn't respond in the group chat, either, so I
assumed they had DM'd her, too.

Now that we weren't filming, I decided to start editing, but just as I
was about to do so, the doorbell rang repeatedly, irritatingly.

"Only one person rings the bell like this."

I sighed and stood up to head for the door.

As I expected, it was Himeji.

"Ryou."

"Could you stop ringing it like that? We're not kids anymo—"

She cut me off with a huge smile, throwing herself at me.

"I passed. I'm in. I got it!"

"Huh? Uh… Whaaa—? Niiice?" I had no idea what she was talking about for a moment and gave a vague reaction, but then I made the connection. "O-oh, wow! That's great, Himeji!"

"I did it! I did it, Ryou! I won!"

She hopped like an excited child.

"Congratulations."

"Yes! And—"

Now Himeji was cut off by the sound of the living room door opening. Himeji jumped away from me, and I heard Mana's voice:

"What's the fuss all about?! Stop shouting at my door!"

"I'm sorry. I just had something to tell him."

"Well, Bubby? Why don't you go listen to her?" She pointed her chin upward.

Go talk in your room—I see.

I asked her to come in. She was still in high spirits.

…So this means that Fushimi didn't…

"So they called my agency first, and I was totally losing my mind when I heard about it from Mr. Matsuda…"

She started flailing her legs just thinking back on it. Kicking my bed was her way of holding in the excitement. Hmm.

"So, who were you rooting for? Hina? Or me?"

"…Both."

"Gosh. You should have said me, even if it wasn't true." She sighed dramatically before putting on a smile again. "Anyway, I wasn't expecting you to be that considerate in the first place, so whatever."

"Hey!"

She beamed even in the face of my grumbling.

"You promised me you'd cheer me on, and I gave it my all with that in mind. I just felt like I needed to thank you, even if just a little."

"Well, it's an honor to have helped you in whichever way possible."

Himeji cleared her throat, trying to regain her composure.

"And since you were *totally* rooting for me, I wanted you to know first. So I rushed all the way here."

"…Thanks?"

Was there a need to say "totally" like that? You totally don't believe I was rooting for you, huh.

Himeji crossed her legs, placed a hand on her chest, and looked me straight in the eye.

"Now that I have passed the audition, you have the right to kiss me."

"What're you talking about?"

"You heard me."

"Why?"

"You have the right."

"…Um. Okay…?" I said suspiciously.

She put on a confident smile. "I know you won't take advantage of it."

"No, I won't."

I didn't ask for such a right in the first place.

"After all, if you ever dared to do so, you'd end up hopelessly falling for me."

How can you be so sure?

"So if you're ever mentally prepared for that, then………" She hesitated to say the rest, her face turning redder and redder with every second. "Then…you can kiss me."

Her confident tone tapered off, her voice becoming quieter. I wouldn't have heard her if we weren't in my silent room.

…Mentally prepared, huh. Mentally prepared to fall in love…

The phrase echoed in my mind; I doubted Himeji had intended for her words to affect me this much.

The conversation ended there. I went down to the kitchen and came back with tea.

"Ryou, did you know about Hina?"

"You mean how she wanted the day off?"

"Yes. I just read the message."

"Since you received the results, I imagine she did as well."

"You think it's because of that?" she asked.

Setting that aside for a moment, did you come all the way to my house unaware that we were supposed to be filming today?

"Apparently, they called everyone to inform them of the results. Mr. Matsuda said that although I passed, they had a few critiques."

They had pointed out stuff about her acting and singing. It was so harsh, one had to wonder if she really passed.

"You usually hear all that from your agent, but considering Hina's working on her own, she must've heard it firsthand."

"Why kick her when she's down...?"

So they told her exactly why she failed.

"A lot of people can't accept the results until they're told why they were rejected."

I immediately thought of visiting her, but what would I even say? Any words of encouragement or consolation I could come up with would only ring hollow.

"I don't think she'd hold a grudge, but I don't know how I should act when I see her again... I think it might be best to just leave her alone for a while."

I nodded. Then Himeji told me about the role she'd be playing.

A few days went by since Fushimi had asked that we postpone the filming. I hadn't heard from her since.

I looked for an excuse to meet and messaged her asking if she could check my homework, but she left me on read.

I felt like she'd usually say yes to that request; she must've been immensely hurt. Or maybe she was actually feeling unwell still? That'd only have me worrying in a different way, though.

Himeji, Torigoe, Mana, and Deguchi, everyone was worried about her. Apparently, she wasn't answering anyone.

It was the day before our next scheduled filming.

I sent a schedule confirmation message to the group chat. Fushimi responded with an OK sticker. *I guess she'll be fine tomorrow.*

I doubted she'd be back in shape right away, but at the very least, we could continue filming.

The day came, and at first glance, she looked the same as always. She cheerfully smiled at everyone. And, well, filming was…not exactly on schedule, but we weren't that behind. All good.

"Thank goodness Hina is feeling better," Torigoe said in between shots in the classroom.

"Yup! I guess it was just a cold or something." Mana also looked relieved.

Fushimi, though not in the highest spirits, was mostly her normal self. Perfect, as always.

"Maybe she wasn't even ill," Himeji said.

"Good job today, everyone!" Deguchi shouted once we wrapped up.

"I have homework to do. See you all." With a smile, Fushimi quickly left.

We had talked about going to eat somewhere all together, but I decided to take my stuff and leave right away, too.

I followed Fushimi and just barely made it on the same train as her. She got on the next car over.

She sat down and stared into space—a shell of a girl. Like an android made in her image.

*Hey, nice job back there. Great acting as always…*felt a bit too distant. *What should I say?*

Hey, I haven't finished my homework yet; how about we do it together? That felt safer, but, I mean, she had already ignored a similar request…

We arrived at our station before I could make up my mind. I got off, but then I realized she hadn't.

"What?"

You're gonna miss the stop, Fushimi! It was then that I heard the announcer's voice, and I got back on the train. The door closed right behind me, and the train departed.

I walked to the next car over. "Fushimi," I finally said.

She turned my way, and her vacant eyes finally seemed to focus, meeting my gaze.

"Ryou."

"You missed our stop."

"Oh… You're right."

I sat down beside her and stared out the window at the view I usually didn't see.

"Your head's in the clouds."

"Hee-hee. You're right. I should be more careful."

I knew that smile.

"You were lying, weren't you?"

"About what?"

"Homework. You don't have any left to do."

"Why do you think that?"

"You always finish in July."

She always helped me out with mine. At least back in every summer of grade school.

"I was just busy this year."

"I sure hope that's it."

Maybe that was one odd thing about her today—having homework left to do in August.

"Remember last time? I made you come with me all the way to the last stop."

"Yeah, I remember."

Although we're going the opposite way this time.

We arrived at the next station, but she showed no intention of getting off.

"So are we going all the way to the end this time, too?"

I had no plans anyway. Didn't need to rush and finish homework, either.

"Yeah. Let's do that," she said.

It wasn't like I had a particular place in mind. Rather, I didn't even know what was around there.

The train got emptier and emptier. I was seeing more and more green and mountains outside the windows.

We finally arrived at the last station—a deserted, tiny place about eighty square feet in size. It was surrounded by mountains and a river on the side.

There was one vending machine outside the station and an old mom-and-pop shop.

"It's so hot. We'll get sunburned."

"Yeah," I said.

We sat down on the bench outside the deserted station and talked about nothing in particular.

Something else felt odd about Fushimi that day, and it kept bothering me.

"Hey, Fushimi, how long do you plan to keep up your facade?"

"Huh?"

"Maybe it's just me?"

"No, Ryou."

"So?"

"I have to keep it up or I'll cry."

She said it with a smile. A pitiful smile.

"I have to, or I'll cause trouble for everyone. I can't keep delaying the filming."

I could think of only one thing that was at the root of all this.

"...I heard about the audition."

"Oh." She was still smiling.

I grabbed her pale cheeks and pulled as hard as I could.

"Hey! Stop that! It hurts!"

"You stop it. Take that smile off your face already. Stop worrying about other people. Trouble them if you have to."

Fushimi's protagonist energy had let her obtain everything she wanted up to now. Any wall that seemed hundreds of feet tall to me, she would climb without breaking a sweat.

Now she had failed.

"Just cry."

"Why...?"

"Don't make yourself smile. Cry if you want to."

"You're asking me to stop smiling? You want me to cry? That's insane..." Tears started welling up, her eyes turning red. "Ryou. Have you seen an Olympic athlete after losing? They always apologize to everyone who cheered them on. And...I feel like that...now."

...So it's only harder on her because she thought I was cheering her on.

Don't worry about me.

To begin with, I'm always the one troubling you.

"You know, Mr. Matsuda told me what you did almost never happens. The auditions are full of the elite, right? People already in agencies, already accepted as professionals. And you made your way to the final screening, beating many of them on the way. That's amazing."

The second and third rounds were about acting and singing, and she had passed those—they recognized her skills.

"No, don't praise me..." Her voice trembled. She tightly pursed her lips.

Mr. Matsuda was right. I was envious of Fushimi's ability that was recognized by other people. Of her having one goal to work toward.

But I also admired her for that.

"And despite your internal turmoil and having postponed filming once, you did perfect today."

"Stop..." She grabbed my sleeve.

But I didn't listen.

"No one noticed something was up. No one was worried about you today. You were perfect." I heard her sniffle. "Isn't that what you'd call a great actress?"

I placed a hand on her head. She started sobbing softly.

"I'm so frustrated..."

I nodded.

"I can't believe it."

I nodded again.

"What can they possibly know about me after just a few tests and interviews?"

"Right?" I rubbed her back.

Her shoulders trembling, she let out a wail.

Fushimi had always been the quickest to cry out of us—Himeji, Mana, and me.

She cried at the slightest sign of loneliness or sadness, but she also cried whenever she was angry, since she was too kind to yell at anyone.

But then, somewhere down the road, Fushimi's expression of sadness had changed; she went from crying to smiling. The one she had showed back at school today was her specialty—a smile that could cover any and all emotion.

"You praise me, but seriously, I'm such a bad girl." *That again?* "You worry about me. You run after me. You comfort me. You're the only one who notices my fake smile... I'm happy about all of this."

"Who wouldn't want to cheer up someone who's feeling bad?"

"Even as I was listening to the results, I was thinking about this in the back of my mind… I knew what I could say to get you to be nice to me…"

Oh, so that's why you kept up the fake smile even when it was just us two, because you didn't want to worry me?

"Is that really bad, though?"

"That's not all. I…I knew you liked Ai, and I tried stealing you from her!" She immediately shut her mouth, as if wishing to take it back.

"…So you wrote that I was going to kiss you once we were in high school?" I asked.

She gave a small, trembling nod.

So that's what really happened.

"I wrote it and then pretended we made the promise together. I also tore the page where you wrote her name…"

Oh yeah, I noticed there was a ripped page.

"And there are many other promises I made up!"

Wait, are you serious? That's pretty bad, actually.

"I was being so, so unfair… I don't deserve your kindness."

Hmm… You think?

"No, you do."

"Huh?" She looked at me, her eyes red from crying.

"You've been helping me a lot, in many ways. I think you rightfully deserve it."

"No. I don't!"

"C'mon."

"I wasn't your best childhood friend, and I wanted to be it so badly."

What was I supposed to say to that? I felt like I blushed a little.

I guess most of what Himeji said was true.

It was a shocking revelation, but not big enough to change the way I saw her. I didn't have the slightest intention of ruining our relationship.

Fushimi kept sobbing for a while, but her tears dried up soon enough.

©Fly

Wrapped up in the sentimentality of the situation, I didn't think anything of it—but why had we traveled all the way to the middle of nowhere? I looked down and saw ants carrying food by my feet. I looked up and saw black kites calmly flying in the sky.

"Let's go home." I stood up.

Fushimi nodded and got up as well.

The announcer's awkward voice played, stating the train's arrival. Far away, the railroad crossing bell rang, and the gate arms went down.

"Hey, Ryou."

"Yeah?"

"I'll just keep on being unfair if you keep saying stuff like that. Is that okay with you?"

"I can't really allow it when you put it like that."

"Whaaa—?! Why the change all of a sudden?!" She pouted impishly.

"From what? I never said anything of the sort." I chuckled.

Then she grinned, something obviously on her mind.

"How about this?!" She jumped and held me tight.

"Hey, let go! The train's coming!"

"Fine!"

She stuck her tongue out before pulling away.

"Hey, Ryou…"

The wheels and rails creaked as the train arrived at the platform.

Then I made just one promise with her.

"So summer break will end eventually." I finally brought up the topic at work.

Mr. Matsuda realized what I meant and tucked in his head. He gave me a wary look.

"S-so?"

"I already bought what I wanted, so once summer break ends—"

"No! Don't say it!" He cut me off before I could tell him I wanted to quit. "You're abandoning me, Ry?!"

"I'm not 'abandoning' you; it's not such a big deal…"

He had switched to calling me "Ry" now. Maybe he just got tired of "Ryo-Ryo," or maybe he just found it too long a nickname.

"You just have to hire someone else."

"What if we can't find a man as good as you?!"

Does it have to be a man?

"Look harder."

"See, hiring people is like pulling a loot box. It is exactly the same."

"Oh, now that's an analogy I can understand."

He had gotten better with handling technology after I told him about this mobile game, which he really got into. Now he was raising idols in real life and within a game.

"A-hem. So, about Fushimi, how's she been doing?"

Don't just change the subject.

"She was really bummed out about failing the audition, but now she seems fine."

We had just made plans to go to the summer festival with everyone.

"I see. That's good. Would you mind telling her to come join my agency if she wants?" He stood up and gave me his business card. "Here, give her this. Tell her to come if she wants to seriously break into the industry."

"Okay."

I put the card away in my wallet so I wouldn't lose it.

"She's good enough to get to the last stage of the audition, and considering she's childhood friends with Aika, maybe we could even make them a unit?"

I tried picturing Fushimi as an idol.

And if she was to form a group with Himeji... I could only picture something out of a shounen manga—rivals joining hands to take down a greater force.

In any case, she didn't seem to have interest in that field. She probably wouldn't do it.

"By the way, did Aika tell you she passed?"

"Yes. She told me the same day you told her."

"I'm glad the director recognized her talent. I'm doubly glad because that also means my judgment was correct."

After filming with her, I realized she had the charm to carry a whole project. She had the star quality, the charisma.

To think I had the opposite impression not so long ago. She must have just lacked the acting experience.

Maybe the person who had selected the winner felt the same way.

Though her charm clashed with her overly high self-esteem...

"She would also be great as a singing actress, not only an idol," Mr. Matsuda said.

"From what I can tell from our film project, I think Fushimi's better."

Mr. Matsuda giggled. "There are lots of skilled and cute girls. But Aika has this special something."

Why ask Fushimi to join the agency if you think that, then?

He correctly guessed what I was thinking and told me that he had high expectations for her future. Something that wasn't taken into account in auditions.

"But you're right, Ry. Aika's still pretty bad."

"Yet she passed."

If Fushimi had better acting skills than Himeji… I wondered if there was another girl who was even better than Fushimi.

"Hopefully you don't find this disappointing, but…," he warned. "They told me on the phone that they liked her history of quitting the idol industry. I mean, the director wasn't big on it, but the producer liked the drama aspect—a girl who ran from the idol field in tears, now return-ing to the stage once again, this time as an actress."

"Did you tell Himeji that?"

"I would never. I can't let her turn it down because of that. You see, this industry, that Aika's already knee-deep in and Fushimi's trying to enter, is a dog-eat-dog world. Sometimes we adults must play dirty."

So technically, Fushimi didn't lose.

I didn't want to dampen Himeji's pure excitement for having won, though, so I erased this whole conversation from my brain.

"Was she happy when she told you about it?"

"Yes, she was beaming."

"I can imagine. So are you rooting for her?"

"Of course."

"Would you help her out if you had the chance?"

I feel like there was something off in the way he phrased that.

"…Yes. If there's anything I can do."

"I was so sure of it when I saw how her expression changed after we ran into you that day." He meant when I'd met her right after seeing Fushimi off for the audition; Himeji was restless up until then. "I felt it would be okay if she fell in love, if she got hurt and cried, if it was with you. She'd be able to use that experience to help further express her emotions. She's too pure as she is now."

He then asked of me:

"That's why, for her sake, I want you to be her boyfriend."

Afterword

Hello, everyone. Kennoji here.

It was around this time last year that quarantine began. It was a huge affair, but since I am a professional shut-in (?), I saw no big changes in my daily life. I sat in a corner, writing all day, like always. And today I continue to live the same life I did back in 2019.

Perhaps not all authors write at home, but I'm the type who can't write while outside. I feel grateful for that now.

You see, I simply can't focus with all the people around at a café or a family restaurant. I like observing people, so my eyes tend to wander for that reason before I even realize it.

Though, when it comes to coming up with ideas for the plot or dialogue, I would say I do that outside most of the time. When trying to do that at my desk, I always end up getting distracted by the lure of my computer or manga that's sitting nearby.

It's funny how the actual writing I have to do at home, though.

Now, the manga version of *The Girl I Saved on the Train* has begun serialization, with weekly updates. I'm sure some of you have already seen it. It's done so well!

Haco Matsuura is really good at structuring the story for the manga, and the characters Yoh Midorikawa draws are extremely cute!

You can check it out on *Manga UP!* so if you haven't given it a look yet, please do.

*   *   *

I also started writing another childhood-friend rom-com published by Sneaker Bunko: *My Childhood Friend Asked Me for Love Advice. It Sounds Like She's Talking About Me, but She Insists That's Not the Case.*

I think any fan of this series would also like that one. I'd greatly appreciate it if you could give it a try.

It is only thanks to the work of many people that this series is made possible.

I want to thank Fly for the exceedingly cute heroine illustrations, and also my editor, and everyone involved in the production of this book, as well as the stores that carry it and their clerks, and, of course, you for reading it. I am deeply grateful.

Look forward to the fifth volume!

KENNOJI

The Girl I Saved on the
Train Turned Out to Be
My Childhood Friend

Kennoji
Illustration by Fly